Not a
Good
Look

Also by Nikki Carter

Step to This
It Is What It Is
It's All Good
Cool Like That

Published by Dafina Books

Not a Good Look

A Fab Life Novel

NIKKI CARTER

KENSINGTON PUBLISHING CORP.

www.kensingtonbooks.com

DAFINA BOOKS are published by

Kensington Publishing Corp.
119 West 40th Street
New York, NY 10018

All Kensington titles, imprints, and distributed lines are available at special quantity discounts for bulk purchases for sales promotion, premiums, fund-raising, educational, or institutional use.

Special book excerpts or customized printings can also be created to fit specific needs. For details, write or phone the office of the Kensington Special Sales Manager: Kensington Publishing Corp., 119 West 40th Street, New York, NY 10018. Attn. Special Sales Department. Phone: 1-800-221-2647.

ISBN-13: 978-0-7582-5556-3
ISBN-10: 0-7582-5556-X

First Printing: September 2010
10 9 8 7 6 5 4 3 2 1

Printed in the United States of America

To my girls and boy ☺

Acknowledgments

I feel so privileged to be able to write these books! I thank God for being able to let my hair down and relive some of my teen days.

My family totally rocks! Thank you, Brent, Briana, Brittany, Brynn, Brooke, and Brent II for eating pancakes for dinner, washing your own clothes, and for giving me quiet Saturdays to finish my stories. I couldn't do this without you!

Thanks to ReShonda Tate Billingsley, Rhonda McKnight, Sherri Lewis, and Dee Stewart—my sista authors who continue to help me promote my teen books! ReShonda, I'ma need you to hurry up and blow up so we can go with you!☺ Thanks to Stephenie Meyer and those *Twilight* books for reminding me of how dramatic we were as teenage girls (Team Edward, all day and all night). Thanks to the Queen Esther Movement, Teenreads.com, and OOSA Online Book Club for your constant plugs!

To my team at Kensington—you are worth so much more than a basket of fruit! Mercedes, you are the business girl! I appreciate everything you do, even when you're harassing me about deadlines; it's all in love . . . I think.

I am blessed to have the best agent ever! Pattie Steele-Perkins, you ROCK! Thank you for talking me down and showing me the ropes of this crazy business.

Thanks to Beyoncé, Jay-Z, Solange, Chrisette Michele, Alicia Keys, and Drake for making hot music that helps me write. Thank you, Mediatakeout.com, Crunktastical.net, Bossip.com, theybf.com, and Sandrarose.com for giving me all the celebrity updates that I need on a daily basis!

To my readers, thank you for your Facebook messages, your random surveys, and quizzes. I enjoy playing Sorority Life with y'all, trying to figure out which Twilight character I am, and debating who has more swagger— Jay-Z or Lil Wayne. Apparently, y'all think it's Lil Wayne. . . .

Thanks for reading, and I hope you enjoy!

Holla!

Nikki

Not a
Good
Look

1

I cannot believe that it's the middle of the night and I'm thirsty. I'm parched, really—my throat feels like it's growing an afro weave.

I glance to the left of me in the dark. I can make out my cousin Dreya's shape in the twin bed on the other side of *my* room. No one can tell it's my room, since I always have to share with Dreya and her little brother, Manny.

They get on my last nerve. Honestly.

Dreya is the reason for my cotton mouth. She finds it necessary to get out of the bed every night and turn the heat up to eighty-five degrees, like she and her mama are paying any bills up in here. Nobody with human blood running through their veins needs to sleep with the heat turned up that high.

And, of course, the vent is right up over my bed. Because of this, I've been swallowing heat for the past few hours.

I throw my feet over the bed and try to escape quietly before . . .

"Sunday! I want some water."

Manny wakes up. Dang!

"Boy, you can't have no water. You're just gonna pee in the bed."

He starts whining. "But I'm thirsty."

"Boy! Go to sleep."

He squints at me and frowns. "What's wrong with yo' throat? You sound like a man!"

"I'm thirsty and my throat is dry!"

"Mine too, so hook a brotha up and get me something to drink."

"Manny, I'm gonna hurt you!"

"I'm gonna tell my mama you cussed at me."

"I did not cuss at you."

"So."

I narrow my eyes at this little evil genius. He stays trying to blackmail somebody. The other day, he got half a candy bar out of Dreya by threatening to tell that she was kissing a dude other than her boyfriend. The fact that she never actually kissed anyone meant absolutely nothing to Manny. A candy bar is a candy bar to that little hobgoblin.

"Come on then," I say, still fussing. "You better not try to get in my bed either."

"I don't even want to sleep in yo' dusty bed! I'm sleeping with my sister!"

Beautiful! The thought of this makes me smile. Dreya's gonna be heated when she wakes up to sheets soaked with Manny's pee! That almost makes up for my interrupted sleep. Ha!

Manny and I creep quietly into the kitchen, which is hard to do because we have to pass through the living room to get there. We tiptoe around feet, legs, and blankets that are spread where they shouldn't be. It's something like a hood slumber party obstacle course.

In most people's homes (I would think—since I really don't go to other people's houses at night) the living room is a pretty quiet place. Living goes on during the day, so that's when it should be busy. At night, normal people go to their bedrooms and go to sleep, and their living room is quiet.

It's a whole other story in the Tolliver household. Our tiny living room is occupied twenty-four seven. My auntie, Charlie, is sleeping on one couch and my mother's boyfriend, Carlos, is asleep on the love seat, wrapped in Manny's *Transformers* comforter.

"Gimme my blanket!" Manny hisses and tries to snatch his comforter from Carlos.

I pull Manny into the kitchen, not wanting him to wake anyone. "Stop it, Manny! You don't have a bed anyway, so it doesn't matter."

"I did at my other house."

"I wish you'd go back to your other house," I mumble under my breath.

Aunt Charlie, Dreya, and Manny moved here a year ago when they got evicted from their duplex. My aunt doesn't keep a job for longer than three weeks, and they never have enough money for rent, so they live with us off and on. It really sucks lemons.

As much as it irritates my mother that Aunt Charlie won't get and stay on her feet, she won't ever let her and her kids be homeless or on the street. That is not how Tollivers roll. We always stick together, no matter what. Even if we get on one another's last nerve.

"Sunday, I'm thirsty. Hurry up," Manny says.

I know he's not trying to have an attitude. Let him keep it up and he'll be swallowing spit.

Just for that, I take my time getting Manny's sippy cup out of the dish rack on the counter and filling it with water from the faucet. I try to hand it to him, but he shakes his head.

"I thought you wanted some water."

He shakes his head again. "Put some ice in it."

"We ain't got no ice."

"Yes, we do. My mama filled up the trays. I saw her."

I open the freezer, crack two ice cubes out of the plastic tray, and drop them into Manny's cup.

While he's drinking, I search in the refrigerator for my orange, pineapple, and banana juice. The fruity goodness that will slide down my throat in a burst of yummy flavor will be the cure for my dry, parched mouth.

I know I sound like a commercial. It was completely intentional. Plus my juice is the bidness, ya dig?

For some reason, I can't seem to find it in our refrigerator. This can only mean one thing. My beloved juice has been stolen and consumed by someone else in this house.

"Manny, who drank my juice?"

He shrugs. "How you expect me to know? I'm only four."

"Because you always asking your mama for my stuff!"

"What color was your juice?"

"What *color* was it? It was yellow!" I feel the anger rising from the pit of my stomach to my dry and crackly throat.

"Oh, that must be the juice I had tonight with my fried bologna sandwich."

AARRRGGGHHHH!!! If my throat didn't feel as dry as the Sahara Desert, I would scream that out loud, but right about now, I can only offer a raspy hiss.

I leave Manny standing there in the kitchen, with his ice water, as I storm back through the living room and down the hall. I can't stand all these people up in me and my mama's spot. I don't have anything to myself, not my own room, my own clothes. Not even a carton of juice. I wish they would all disappear!

Then I hear whimpering coming from the kitchen.

I roll my eyes and go back to get Manny. "How you gon' have all that mouth and be scared of the dark?"

"I'm not scared of the dark. I'm scared of roaches."

"We don't have roaches, Manny."

"We did at the other house."

I sigh and scoop him up into my arms. "Just come on."

I tuck Manny into the bed with Dreya and get back in my bed. I close my eyes and try to go back to sleep.

Which is impossible.

Because. I'm. Still. Thirsty!

2

*"I wish my whole life was a fantasy / keep waiting
for someone to wake me."*
—Sunday Tolliver

I open my eyes and wake up to the same thing I wake up
to every morning. Chaos.

"Manny, you better not sleep in my bed again, with
your Peabody behind."

I snicker into my pillow. Dreya and Aunt Charlie call
Manny "Mr. Peabody" whenever he wets the bed. If you
ask me, it's mean, but I don't get into their immediate-
family drama.

"Sunday, where are your gold hoop earrings? I need
them for my outfit."

Why is it that none of Dreya's outfits are complete
without borrowing something of mine? My gold hoops
don't even go with what she has on—layered tank tops
with a short leather jacket, skinny jeans, and black leather
ankle boots. She looks like a biker chick, and biker chicks
should be rocking chains—not my earrings.

"I don't know where they are."

That was a total lie. I know exactly where my real 18-karat gold earrings are. The ones I got from my ex-boyfriend, Romell, on my sixteenth birthday. The ones I hardly ever take off. They are in a box under my pillow.

Wanna know where they're not going? In Dreya's multi-pierced ears.

Dreya sucks her teeth and runs her hand through her short hair. "You're such a liar."

Once upon a time Dreya used to have long, thick hair like me, but she decided that it would look better if one side was shaved. The unshaved part has blond tips and is styled in an unruly roller set. She thinks it looks hawt . . . I guess as long as she likes it, that's the most important thing.

"Sunday, get up and get ready for school!"

My mother is standing in the doorway, wearing her postal uniform, somehow managing to make the plain blue and gray pants and shirt look fly. Her hands are on her hips as if she's going to do something other than yell to get me out of bed.

"Is Aunt Charlie still in the shower? Because if she is, I can sleep for ten more minutes."

"Yeah, my mommy is still in the shower, and what?" Manny says while standing at the foot of my bed wearing only his pajama top.

How's he gonna have an attitude problem and still be peeing in the bed?

I throw a pillow at him. He's always trying to have his mama or his sister's back when they're the ones always spanking his little behind.

My mother sucks her teeth and grabs the bottom of my blanket, trying to pull it away.

"She'll be out in a minute, Sunday. Get on up and get your stuff together because Carlos needs to get in there, too."

It makes no sense that the two people in this house who have absolutely nothing to do all day would need to be in my way when it's time to get dressed. Aunt Charlie isn't even thinking about a job, and none of Carlos's business associates are up this early. I use the term *business associates* loosely because, on the real, don't you have to be making money from something for it to be called *business?*

Other than his failure to generate income, Carlos is cool people. Out of all the boyfriends my mom has kicked it with, he's the best one. He makes my mother laugh, and he doesn't try to act like my daddy. Every now and then we'll play a video game or two on Xbox and chill.

My mother sees my eyes roll and says, "Sunday, I know what you're thinking. Carlos has a stock-options-trading class this morning. My baby is about to get into the stocks and bonds market."

I roll my eyes again and throw myself out of the bed. Carlos always has something going that's about to take off. Two months ago, it was a check-cashing store, six months ago it was a Laundromat that had a bunch of half-broken washing machines and dryers. Needless to say, it didn't pan out. And until one of his ideas makes him some money, he's gonna be my mother's boyfriend and not her husband. She claims she's not marrying him until he can take care of us.

I'm waiting to see if that's gonna happen. It wouldn't be a bad thing at all because, like I said, Carlos is good people. But I'm not holding my breath, or getting my hopes up.

As soon as I hear the water in the shower shut off and the bathroom door open, I dash in with all my Bath & Body Works toiletries and my outfit. Before all these people moved up in our crib, I could leave my stuff in the bathroom. Not so, anymore. Aunt Charlie and Dreya used up a whole bottle of Sweet Pea lotion in one day. What do you know? The water is cold. It's okay, though, because I love taking cold showers in the fall. Sarcasm in full effect.

Strands from Aunt Charlie's platinum blond yaki weave are all over the shower curtain and clogging up the drain, causing the chilly water to rise up around my feet. I let out a long sigh and wash myself quickly, because I really am running late.

After I'm dressed in a bebe tee and Apple Bottoms jeans, I slick my hair into a bun with a long, curly side bang in the front. My gold hoop earrings and grape lip gloss complete the look. Yes, *my* gold hoop earrings.

When I finally emerge from the bathroom, my best friend, Bethany, is in the living room harmonizing with Dreya on a song that I wrote. I should say that they are attempting to harmonize, because Dreya doesn't harmonize. She can sing the mess out of a solo, but getting her voice to blend with other voices is a pretty tough task.

Bethany must be able to tell that there's something not right about their vocals because she twirls her thick, brown cornrows between her fingers. Nobody likes to tell Dreya she hit a wrong note, especially not Bethany. She looks away from Dreya and slides her hand over the words on her baby tee and into her snug jeans pocket.

Bethany is cool as what. We've been girls since elementary school. We have the occasional beef, but she's a down type chick, and she can sing.

Even if she competes with me over boys.

Dreya, Bethany, and I are a girl singing group called Daddy's Little Girls. The name was Dreya's idea, and since I do write all the songs, the least I could do was let her name the group.

"You're flat, Dreya," I say, as my cousin tries unsuccessfully to hit another string of notes.

Dreya puts her hand on her hip and gives me the stank attitude look. "Hi, hater. You're just mad because my runs are off the chain."

"I don't know about off the chain, but they *are* off. Actually, every time you do a run, you go flat. You've got to learn better voice control, Dreya. When was the last time you sang scales?"

"Whatever, Sunday. Who made you vocal instructor? Oh, and I see you conveniently found your earrings," Dreya says as she flicks one of my earrings with her hand.

I reply, "Imagine that."

Bethany laughs. "As if she'd ever lose them. Her boo gave her those."

"Romell is not my boo," I protest.

"Yes, he is," Bethany teases.

"No. Romell is a cheater. And that's why you look like Ice-T's wife, Coco, with them cornrows to the back."

Clearly, I'm trying to deflect attention away from the conversation about cheater Romell and onto Bethany's hip-hop look. Although I just clowned her, the cornrows actually suit her dainty, pretty face, pulling her wide eyes into slants that make her dark eyelashes even more striking. Glitter lip gloss completes her look.

Bethany giggles. "I love it when you get all angry, Sunday. Anyway, Coco's boobs are bigger than mine."

"Are we rehearsing after school or what?" Dreya asks as she grabs her backpack. "Truth is outside."

"Yeah, because y'all most definitely need it," I reply.

Carlos chuckles from the kitchen.

"What are *you* laughing at?" Dreya asks.

"You could use a lil' work, Dreya," Carlos replies. With his thick Puerto Rican accent, he almost rolls the *r* in Dreya's name.

"Ugh. Why don't you just make your pancakes?" Dreya says with attitude.

The fact that Dreya and Carlos don't get along makes him even cooler in my book. He laughs her off and flips a plate-sized pancake on the skillet.

My mother storms up the hallway from her bedroom. She looks really mad about something as she snatches her keys and purse and walks toward the door.

Carlos calls from the kitchen, "You not gonna say 'bye or wish me luck on my class?"

Maybe after dating my mother for two years, Carlos still can't read her moods. But I wasn't even about to trip about her leaving without a word, because I can tell she's heated about something. I'd help a brotha out, but I ain't trying to get in my mama's warpath.

She spins around with fire in her eyes. "Carlos, you really need to check your baby mama."

He blows breath through his lips in an irritated-sounding whistle. "Did LaKeisha call you again? What did she want?"

"The same thing she always wants, Carlos. Money. She said your son needs some new sneakers."

Carlos sighs. "Okay. I'll call her back."

"When you talk to her, tell her to lose my number."

Carlos walks over to my mother and pulls her into a hug. "I'm so sorry, Shawn. I'll handle it."

Just like that her anger melts away and the fire leaves her eyes. Carlos's got some serious skills, because I thought she was going to flip out on him.

My mom looks at the three of us girls all up in their business. She narrows her eyes at Carlos, like she wants to say more but doesn't want to say it in front of us.

"I'm going to work, Carlos. We'll talk about it when I get home."

My mom slams the door as she leaves and Carlos goes back to fixing his breakfast.

"Come on, Bethany," I say. "This is too much drama this early in the morning."

Bethany, Dreya, and I walk outside. Me and Bethany are on our way to the bus stop, but Dreya's grown, nineteen-year-old boyfriend, Truth, is waiting for her in his tricked-out Impala. You would think they'd offer us a ride since we're all going to the same school, but nope—they're not even cool like that.

As Bethany and I start down the street, my cell phone rings. "Hello."

"Sunday, it's Dreya."

I whip my head around to see if they're still parked in front of the house, but they've already pulled off.

"What's up?" I ask.

"I can't practice after school because I'm going to the studio with Truth. He's almost done with his album and he wants me there for inspiration."

"All right then. Me and Bethany will practice without you."

Bethany looks at me with questions in her eyes as I press End on my phone.

"What?" she asks.

"Dreya's not practicing after school."

"What's new? She hardly ever practices—that's why she sounds a mess."

"I know. We're never gonna get a record deal, messing around with her."

"You're going to college anyway. It's not like you'll be able to go to school and be a star."

"If we get a record deal between now and the time we graduate, I can help my mom pay my college bills."

"Or you could not go to school," Bethany says. "Then we could kick it hard on the red carpets and go on tour and . . ."

This is the part where I tune Bethany out. Truth is, I don't really want to be a star. I want to be rich, not famous. And as far as being an artist is concerned, I want to write songs. I couldn't care less about being a performer.

But it seems like the way to make all that happen is with a girl group. Here in ATL there are so many retired and semiretired R & B stars looking for the next group to manage or sign. We've been approached by more than one bootleg producer, but I refuse to go out like that.

"Maybe we should ask Dreya if we can come to the studio tonight. You never know what might happen," Bethany says.

"You can ask her. She'll tell me no."

The bus stop is packed, as usual, because everybody is too lazy to walk to school and it's starting to get chilly. October is hit-or-miss down here in the A. It's either warm and sunny or chilly and rainy. Since it's a week away from November, we're getting some of the latter.

I see my ex-boyfriend, Romell, chilling with some of his boys, and butterflies dance in the pit of my stomach. As much as I can't stand him anymore, I still have to admit that he's fine. He's deep, dark chocolate with a pretty smile. His cornrows to the back look good on him, too. But I wonder which new chick put them in for him. His playa tendencies are what made me sideline our teenage love affair.

"Look at your boy," Bethany whispers.

"I ain't thinking about him."

"Then why you still rocking those earrings?"

"Maybe because they're the only piece of jewelry I own that doesn't come from Claire's."

Bethany grins at me like she knows something that I don't. "Whatever, Sunday. You still dig Romell."

I shake my head and click on my iPod. I let the smooth vocals of Chrisette Michele drown out the noise. This girl can blow, for real. Not like these pop princess divas who need Auto-Tune to make a record. My eyes close and my head bobs as I let the music take me to another place where cheating ex-boyfriends don't reside.

Bethany taps me on my shoulder, snapping me out of my trance. "The bus is here."

I nod and follow the rest of the group to the bus. I just listened to a sad song, and it's sticking with me right now. Music does that to me. I can listen to a Jay-Z track and get pumped about my career, or listen to a Biggie track and have to dance no matter what. Seriously, can you hear "Hypnotize" in the club and *not* get up and dance? That's for real.

Bethany usually sits with me on the bus, but today it's packed and we have to split up. I end up sitting in front of Romell, and next to someone who's on their way to work. It would be nice if our school had actual school buses. They just give us bus tickets and expect us to share the public transportation with all the grown people who don't have cars.

I get ready to flick my iPod back on, when Romell leans forward and whispers, "You looking real nice today, Sunday. When're we getting back together?"

Part of me wants to smile because he appreciates my look, but the other part wants to dead that noise because he played me.

"Romell, I'm not getting back with you. You know what it is."

He chuckles, " 'You da you da best / you da you da best.' "

"You can sing all the Drake songs you want, Romell. It's not gonna work. I'm never getting back with you."

"Never?" Romell replies with a laugh. "How you gon' challenge me like that and think I'm not gonna accept?"

A challenge? Wow, I don't even know how he got a challenge out of *I'm never getting back with you*. That's crazy.

"Romell, ain't nobody trying to challenge you. Go holla at Chantelle. She's the one you with now, right? She braid your hair?"

"You like my hair, baby? Thank you, but Chantelle is just for playing—you know that. You're the one I wanna be with."

"Yeah, well, won't Chantelle do whatever you want?"

"She's *too* easy and I'm a man, baby. I like to hunt for my food."

I roll my eyes, flick on my iPod, and hope that Romell can't see the tiny smile on my lips. Yeah, he's a cheater and all, but dang, he's wearing that swagger like Roca-wear cologne.

Wait, did I say I was over him? Well, I am, but a girl can still appreciate fineness. I'm just sayin'.

3

————

Bethany squeezes my arm as we get out of Truth's car in front of the studio. She had begged and pleaded with Dreya for us to be able to come, and Truth had picked us all up from school. Dreya promised us that it was the first and last time that we'd ever be in her man's ride and she threatened Bethany with a slow and painful beat down if she tried to push up on Truth.

"Y'all can sit down over there," Truth directs us as we walk through the studio doors.

Dreya looks hesitant to let her man's hand go when we see three chicks walk by us wearing bathing suits.

"Who are they?" Dreya asks.

Truth grins and his mid-back-length locs move, emphasizing his amusement. He walks up really close to Dreya and kisses her on the neck. While he's doing this, I notice he has a new tattoo on his arm—a microphone. In a minute he's not gonna have anywhere else to add any tattoos; his chocolate brown skin is covered in ink.

"You jealous, ma?" Truth asks.

Dreya sticks her chin out defiantly, like a little kid. "No, never that. I was just wondering why they walkin' around half-naked like it's summertime, and it's cold outside."

"They are doing a photo shoot. They're some little girl singing group. Kinda like y'all, but they can't blow like y'all can."

Kinda like us? That's really funny. There is no way in the world anyone's gonna ever see me doing a photo shoot with no clothes on. That's for no-talent chicks.

Truth continues, "I'm gonna go 'head downstairs 'cause I'm already late. Y'all can chill and watch TV, and somebody will probably come up and get y'all something to eat. You straight with that, wifey?"

Dreya nods and returns Truth's kiss. He untangles himself from her and dashes down a flight of stairs. Dreya looks like she wants to follow him, but she doesn't. She sits down on a leather couch and we follow her.

"Y'all betta not embarrass me up here, especially you, Bethany, with your thirsty self," Dreya says.

I guess I'm looking real lame right now, because I brought my homework, but whatever. I've got a calc test tomorrow, and I don't flunk for nobody. I don't care if they do have a record deal.

This is a pretty fly spot, for real. There's a big flat-screen TV on the wall, surround sound, and theatre chairs. Somebody spent some serious cheddar on this spot.

Just as I finish up my homework, a pretty, brown,

video-vixen type walks into the room. She's got a lace front wig that hangs nearly to her waist, fake eyes, fake boobs, and probably a fake behind, but at least she's fully dressed. I wonder what she looked like before the enhancements.

"Y'all want something to eat?" she asks.

Dreya looks her up and down. "Who are you?"

The girl laughs. "You must be Truth's little girlfriend."

"I'm his wifey."

I have to swallow the laugh that threatens to explode out of my throat. Dreya is hilarious without even trying. As if a girl who looks like this chick would be interested in Truth's broke, on the come-up self. Dreya sounds really desperate right now.

"Well, I'm the receptionist, baby girl, and the hospitality committee. Do you want something to eat or not? We've got lasagna and pound cake in the kitchen."

My eyebrows lift involuntarily. She just said the magic word for me. Lasagna is one of the world's most perfect foods.

"I don't know about her," I say while holding on to my grumbling stomach, "but I'm hungry. I would love some lasagna."

Dreya cuts her eyes at me like she wishes they were a knife. It's whatever. I haven't eaten since lunch and it's dinnertime.

The vixen smiles at me. "Well, come on then. Big D said to roll out the red carpet for y'all."

"Who's Big D?" Bethany asks.

"He's the man who owns this studio."

"Are you his girlfriend?" Dreya asks.

"Something like that."

I don't wait for Dreya to make up her mind about whether or not this girl is a threat. I'm hungry and the scent of freshly baked lasagna has made its way to my nose.

When Bethany stands up, too, Dreya reluctantly joins us. We follow the vixen down the hall, and for real, her butt has to be fake. Each cheek is moving like it has its own personality. Those kinds of booties don't grow naturally, do they?

The vixen girl shows us to the kitchen nook area where we slide into a booth. Dreya's mean mug is slowly evaporating as the girl serves us hot, steaming plates of cheesy lasagna.

"What's your name?" I ask the girl, tired of thinking of her as the vixen in my head.

"It's Michelle, but everybody calls me Shelly."

"Nice to meet you. I'm Sunday, and this is Dreya and Bethany. We're a singing group."

"That's cute," she says. "I used to sing, too, but that was a long time ago."

"So what do you do now? Dance in videos?" Dreya asks.

"No, sweetie. Big D takes good care of me. I don't have to shake my behind in videos to make money."

Bethany's eyes widen. "That's what I'm talkin' 'bout. I need a man like that."

Michelle laughs out loud. "You're a baby. You don't need a man at all."

Thank you, big-donk girl, for spitting knowledge in

the atmosphere! Sometimes I really don't know about Bethany. Some of the stuff she says is twisted.

"If y'all want some more, it's on the stove," Michelle says. "I'm going back downstairs."

"Are we allowed down there?" Bethany asks.

"Maybe. I'll ask, and if they want y'all to sit in on the session, someone will come upstairs and get you."

Michelle jiggles out of the kitchen and leaves us there to finish our food. Stripper or not, she knows what the heck she's doing in the kitchen. This lasagna is the bomb, for real!

"She looks like she stinks," Dreya says.

"Hi, hater," Bethany replies with a giggle.

"Seriously!" Dreya exclaims. "How can you wipe a booty that big?"

"Ewww, you nasty," I say. "Leave me alone so I can eat my food."

"I don't want nothing that booty girl fixed," Dreya says.

"Okay, you can starve then."

Bethany and I scarf down our lasagna and soda like we haven't eaten in weeks, while Dreya watches.

"Didn't she say something about some pound cake?" Bethany asks.

Just when Bethany and I are about to go in search of dessert, a teenage boy comes into the kitchen. He stops in the doorway of the kitchen, leans on the wall, and checks each one of us out.

"Y'all wanna come downstairs?" he asks.

Dreya stands up. "Yeah. It's about time."

The boy looks at Dreya's untouched plate of food. "You didn't like the lasagna?"

"I don't eat food cooked by strippers."

The boy looks offended. "I'm not a stripper!"

I burst into laughter. "I don't know who you are, but, boy, you put your foot in that lasagna."

"I'm Sam, the studio engineer and junior producer. I also like to cook."

"I'm Sunday, this is my girl Bethany, and the hungry chick over there is Dreya."

Sam smiles at me, and I smile back, although he's far from a hottie. His clothes are fresh and his haircut is nice, but he's barely cute with his big nose and lips. He's got a great smile, though, and since I'm not looking for a boyfriend, that's good enough for me.

We follow Sam downstairs to the studio area. Shelly is chilling on a couch reading a book. Truth is in the booth with a headset on, and I guess Big D is the one at the control panel. I've never met Big D, but the giant medallion of the letter _D_ across his chest is a giveaway.

"Which one of you young ladies is Truth's girl?" Big D asks.

Dreya pipes up, "That would be me."

"Well, you betta talk to your man. He needs to finish up this album and he ain't belting out this hook the way I need him to. Sing it again, Truth, while your wifey's down here."

Big D hits some buttons on the control panel and a loud, pulsing beat blazes through the room. My head involuntarily starts to bob, and a melody forms itself around the bass line.

Truth opens up his mouth and sings in a gravelly tenor. His singing voice isn't bad, but the melody is lacking. The one I'm thinking of is a lot hotter, and more fitting for the beat. Obviously, Big D isn't feeling it either because he turns off the music.

He fusses into the microphone leading to the booth. "Truth, man. Come on."

I clear my throat and tap Big D on the shoulder. Dreya's eyes widen like she wants to strangle me, but it's whatever. He needs to hear what I have to say if he wants to make this track hot.

"You interrupting me, right now?" Big D asks.

He sounds irritated, but I'm not scared, because I know he's gonna be pleased when he hears what I have to say.

"I think I can help. The hook you've got him singing doesn't really fit the track."

"You got something better?"

I nod.

"Then let's hear it."

Big D turns the track back on, but waves at Truth to let him know he shouldn't sing. I close my eyes, open my mouth, and sing the lyrics I just freestyled to the track.

"You say I'm the best now show and prove / If I'm the one then make your move / I'm a lady, I'm not sweating you / now what ya gonna do, what ya gonna do?"

I repeat the hook a few times while the track plays, and on the second time, Dreya and Bethany harmonize with me. We sound hot! I'm so proud of them, especially Dreya, because she doesn't go flat even though she does a little run at the end.

Big D claps his hands together. "All right, baby! Now

we talkin'. That's gonna be a hit right there. Wifey, go get in the booth with your man and belt that out."

What? Did everyone not hear me freestyle and lead that hook? Is it my imagination or does he really want Dreya to sing on the track? What in the . . .

"She's got a little bit more flava to her," Big D explains. "You look kinda Disney, sweetheart. We can use her in the video. But you and this whooty right here can sing backup."

Disney! I look *Disney?* I am beyond annoyed as I watch Dreya sashay into the booth and put the headset on. Big D hits the track again and she nails it on the first time. Her soprano sounds pretty good, like Ashanti with a little bit more soul.

"Can I at least get a songwriter credit on the track?" I ask.

Sam grins and Bethany's eyes widen. I wonder if I'm asking for too much. Well, it's too late now. I can't take it back.

"Naw, baby, this is a jam session, so it's like a collabo. But I'll put your name in the thank-you's. How 'bout that?"

Okay, I know how it works in the industry. I know on my first few hits I probably won't get any songwriter credit, or money for that matter. But once I get known for being a hit maker, the paper will come.

Still, I don't like the idea of coming up with an idea and someone else putting their name on it. That sucks, for real, especially since I can't even sing on the track except in the background.

Big D gives me a fist pound. "What's your name, lil' mama? You a real business woman, ain't you?"

"Sunday Tolliver."

"All right then, Ms. Sunday, you keep doing what you doing, and I'ma be writing you checks. That's fo' sho'."

I give Big D a nod and a tight smile. "That's what's up."

"Come on over here, Sam, and do your magic," Big D says.

Sam sits down at the controls, makes a few adjustments, and then gives Dreya and Truth the signal to start again. They go through the entire song, and the track is bumping. Dreya's vocals leave a little to be desired, but it's whatever. Me and Bethany are dancing like we're in the club, and even the laid-back Shelly is getting her groove on.

"That's it right there, Daddy," Shelly says to Big D.

Big D pats me on my back and gives me a fist pound. "I think we've found a little gold mine."

Is he talking about the song or is he talking about me?

4

After the recording session, Dreya decided to play wifey and stayed with Truth at the studio, leaving me and Bethany to find our own ride to the house. Luckily, Sam is on his way out.

"Can we ride with you?" Bethany asks.

"Sure, but I have to make a stop first."

My face tightens. "What kind of stop?"

I'm not about to get caught up in anyone's illegal activities. So if he's making *that* kind of stop, I'll catch a cab.

"I need to get an apple juice slush at Sonic. Is that all right with you?" There's a little gleam in Sam's eye that makes me think he knew what I was thinking.

"Yeah, an apple juice slush is cool."

Bethany and I follow Sam to his car. I watch Bethany graze his body with hers every opportunity she gets. She stays in groupie mode all day and all night. Sam's not even a star, but something on him must smell like swagger.

Sam walks around to the passenger side of his car, a red Explorer SUV, and opens the front door for me. I guess he's not impressed by Bethany and all that junk she's carrying in her trunk, because clearly he wants me riding shotgun. And the door-opening gets him extra points with me.

Bethany looks a tad bit salty, but she climbs in the backseat when Sam opens the door for her as well. I give him the eye as he walks around to his side, and on second appraisal, he's not that bad looking. He's wearing black-framed glasses (not sunglasses, regular glasses) and now has on an Atlanta Falcons cap pulled down low. It's a quirky look, like Lupe Fiasco or somebody, but he working it.

"So where do y'all stay?" Sam asks as he starts the SUV.

"Decatur, off of Candler."

He nods and pulls out of the driveway. I wait to see if he's got any opinion about where we stay. It's not the hood, but it definitely ain't the lavish life. But Sam's face isn't giving anything away, so if he's got an opinion, he's keeping it to himself.

Sam drives into the Sonic at the end of the street and pulls into a parking spot. "Y'all want something?"

"Yeah, I want a cherry limeade slush and Tator Tots," Bethany says.

"And for you, Sunday?" Sam asks.

"Nothing. No, thank you."

"You sure?" he asks.

"Yeah, I'm sure."

Sam shrugs and says, "Okay, fair enough. Maybe next time."

Next time? There's going to be a next time?

Sam orders the drinks and Tater Tots for Bethany. I almost change my mind and order a drink, too, but I'm really not thirsty.

"Sam, how'd you start working for Big D?" Bethany asks.

"A friend told him about my skills, and I went into the studio one day and showed him what I was working with. Next thing you know, I'm the main studio engineer and I'm producing tracks."

"You're so good at it," Bethany says. "I bet you could be making a lot of money if you had your own spot."

"One day, I guess. Right now, Big D pays me well and I'm making a lot of connections."

The Sonic girl brings the order out to the car, and Sam pays her. He watches the girl as she walks away.

"You like what you see?" I ask.

Sam laughs. "I'm sorry. In the summer she always wears short shorts. I guess I was just reminiscing."

I shake my head. Boys are disgusting. Even if they do know how to open car doors and bake lasagna.

I lean back in my seat, intent on being quiet the rest of the way to the house.

"How's it feel to make your first hit?" Sam asks when we stop at a red light.

"It was easy."

Sam chuckles. "That was easy to you, coming up with a hook? Where have you been all my life?"

"I don't know. Are you working with some artists?"

"A few, but nobody with that *it* factor, you know. Just the same ole same ole. Nobody that's gonna blow up. Except Truth. He's gonna be off the charts."

"Do you think we can blow up?" Bethany asks from the backseat.

Sam glances in the rearview mirror and nods. "Y'all definitely could."

"You still in school?" I ask Sam.

"Yeah. I'm a senior at DSA."

"DeKalb School of the Arts?" I ask. "That's hot. You must be talented for real."

Sam blushes a little. I guess I'm embarrassing him. The fact that he's blushing is actually kind of cute, because at least he doesn't have a big head.

"I sing and play piano and cello," he replies.

"Cello?" Bethany falls out laughing in his backseat. "Are you serious?"

I roll my eyes. "Don't listen to her. I love stringed instruments. That's cool."

"Do you play?"

"Nah, but I wish I did. I took a few piano lessons when I was little, but my mom couldn't afford to keep them up. I think it would really help me with my songwriting if I knew how to play."

"I give lessons."

I laugh out loud. "Are they free lessons? I'm trying to go to college, so I don't have a lot of extra cash lying around. Actually, I don't have *any* extra cash lying around."

"For you, they're free."

"Are you flirting with me?" I ask. "Trying to get at me with some piano lessons?"

"Nope. I just think you're talented."

I'm cheesing now, from ear to ear. "Okay, then. Oh, wait. Turn right—this is Bethany's street."

Sam turns onto her street, and asks, "Which one is your house?"

"Second one on the left," Bethany replies. "The red one."

Why is her voice dripping with attitude? Obviously Sam is not checking for her, so she might as well get dropped off first. But I know I'm gonna hear about this tomorrow. She has this thing about claiming boys, whether they're digging her or not.

Sam pulls into Bethany's driveway and she gets out. " 'Bye, Sam. It was nice meeting you."

"Same here."

"See you tomorrow, Bethany," I call as she walks away without saying good-bye to me.

Sam waits until she gets into the house and then backs down her driveway. "She mad at you about something?" he asks.

"Probably. It's whatever, though. She'll get over it."

"So which way do I go to get to your house?"

"Oh. Take a left at the stop sign, and then down the hill."

At the bottom of the hill, in front of my house, are about six police cars. Lights flashing and everything. There's an ambulance and a fire truck, too, which puts me in straight panic mode. I almost lose it when I see my mother standing in our yard crying, with Aunt Charlie holding her up.

"This your house?" Sam asks.

"Yeah, let me out."

I run toward my house and a police officer grabs my arm and tries to stop me. "Young lady—"

"This is my house! That's my mother!"

"It's all right, officer, sir. She lives here." This is Sam talking. I didn't even know he followed me.

"Well, move it indoors, then. There's nothing to see out here."

Sam nods in agreement. "Yes, sir."

The police officer lets go of my arm, and Sam and I run over to my mother.

"Mama, what's wrong?"

My mother opens her mouth to say something, I guess, but then she just breaks down crying.

"Someone shot Carlos."

My eyes open wide. "What? No way!"

"I'm riding to the hospital with him, Sunday," my mother says between sobs. "Just go in the house and stay inside, okay. In case they come back."

"In case who comes back?" I ask frantically. "Do you know who did this?"

My mother kisses my cheek and runs to the ambulance to ride with Carlos to the emergency room.

I turn to Aunt Charlie for answers. "What is going on?"

"He was meeting up with some guys to buy into a club. One of the guys is LaKeisha's brother."

"His baby's mother, LaKeisha?" I ask.

"Yeah. I guess a fight broke out and they followed him back here to finish things off."

"Finish things off? Is Carlos . . ."

Tears well up in Aunt Charlie's eyes. "They shot him so many times that I don't see how he can make it. But God is able."

It must be bad if Aunt Charlie is talking about God. She's one of those people who only thinks of religion, God, and church when she's in some kind of trouble. My chest tightens at the thought of us losing Carlos.

Aunt Charlie looks Sam up and down. "Who are you? And where is Dreya?"

"Dreya stayed with her boyfriend, Aunt Charlie—and this is Sam. He just gave me a ride home from the studio."

"What do you mean, Dreya stayed with her boyfriend?"

I shrug. "I don't know, Aunt Charlie. Where's Manny?"

"Will you go in the house and check on him for me? I'm gonna drive your mother's car to the hospital."

Even though I want to go to the hospital to be with my mother, I nod and obey Aunt Charlie. Sam follows me to the door.

"Are you going to be all right?" Sam asks. "Do you need me to stay?"

Wow. He looks like he's concerned for real, and I've only known him a few hours. I'm touched.

"Could you, please? Just for a little while. I don't know if I want to be here by myself."

"I can stay for as long as you need me to stay."

"Do you have to call someone?" I ask. I don't want him to get in trouble trying to make sure I'm okay.

"My mother works nights. She doesn't come in until after I've already gone to school."

"Okay, well, I just wanna warn you, this isn't a mansion. We're just a regular hood family."

Sam shakes his head. "Sunday . . . why do you think I would care about that?"

"I'm just sayin'."

Truth is, I'm embarrassed about our little house. It's clean and everything, but it's definitely not ready for entertaining. I never have company. In fact, the only people at school who've been here are Bethany and Romell.

I show Sam into the living room, where Aunt Charlie's blankets are still on the couch in front of the television. Her ashtray is filled with several smoking cigarette butts, which I snatch and throw in the garbage.

"You can have a seat here," I say, pointing to the love seat that is blanket free. "Aunt Charlie would trip if she came back and you were sitting on her bed."

Sam sits down. "This is better anyway, because you'll have to sit closer to me."

"Look at you getting fresh!" I say with a tiny giggle. "I could always sit at the table."

"Or we could sit in your bedroom," Sam suggests.

"Now you're tripping," I reply, my tone now all business.

Sam raises two hands in defeat. "I'm joking, Sunday. Calm down."

Manny walks up from the back hallway with a frown on his face, and all that mean mugging is directed straight at Sam. Manny takes that whole "don't talk to strangers" rule to a whole other level.

"Who are you?" Manny asks. He looks angry but his face is streaked with tears.

"I'm Sam. What's up with you, lil' dude?"

"I ain't yo' lil' dude. You don't even know me like that."

I stifle a laugh at the look on Sam's face. He obviously didn't know that Manny was gangsta wit' it.

"Sam, this is my cousin Manny. He's Dreya's little brother."

Sam smiles. "Oh, I'm sorry, sir. You must be the man of this house."

"Yeah. Don't get it twisted, knucklehead. What you doin' here and ain't no grown people home? My auntie don't let no boys be all posted up in her spot like that."

Sam laughs out loud and looks at me. "How old is he?"

"Four going on thirty-five. He watches way too much TV."

"Hey, I can hear y'all," Manny fusses.

"I'm sorry, little man," Sam says. "Some scary stuff happened tonight, and I'm just staying here with y'all until your mother and auntie come back. Is that all right with you?"

Manny gathers his blanket around his shoulders. "It was scary. I heard a gun."

"I'm scared, too, Manny." I scoop Manny up and hug him to my chest.

Manny throws his arms around my neck and squeezes hard. He might think he's four going on thirty-five, but he's just a baby. I kiss his forehead and lay him down on the couch.

Suddenly, I feel kind of open, like Sam is up in my personal space way too quickly. He's got a caring look on his face, but it kind of makes me nervous because we just met.

"Do you want something to drink?" I ask.

Sam holds up his Sonic cup. "No thanks. I still haven't finished my apple slush."

"Okay." I grab the remote control and turn on the TV, hoping that the noise is a distraction.

Sam pats the seat next to him. "Chill, Sunday. You seem completely stressed out. Everything's gonna be all right."

As I sit down, he takes the remote from me and changes the channel to *Meet the Browns*. Even though I never watch sitcoms, I totally could use the distraction.

"Looks like there's a marathon on. Six back-to-back episodes. You down?" Sam asks.

"Sure, whatever."

I try not to laugh, but the combination of Mr. Brown and Sam imitating Mr. Brown gives me a serious case of the giggles. It's definitely helping me to not think about Carlos getting shot.

I stretch my arms toward the ceiling and yawn. I'm tired, but I don't want to go to bed and leave Sam sitting up here by himself watching TV, so I force my eyes to stay open for as long as I can.

I guess Sam and I watched the show until I fell asleep. The only reason I know I fell asleep is because Aunt Charlie taps my leg to wake me.

"Wake up, Sunday. Walk your friend out."

"Wh-what happened with Carlos?"

"They don't know if he's gonna make it. His mama and sister are up at the hospital, too."

I shake my head. "How's my mother doing?"

"She was cool until LaKeisha showed up at the hospital starting mess."

"Why would she even come up there?"

Aunt Charlie shrugs. "I guess seeing if Carlos died or not, because her brother is about to get charged with either murder or attempted murder."

"So y'all know it was him?"

"Who else would it be? The cops said they were getting a warrant for his arrest, so it's only a matter of time."

"This is too messed up," I say.

"Mmm-hmm. That's why we keep telling y'all to go to college, so you don't have to fool with this mess right here."

"I know that's right, Auntie."

"Your boyfriend is waiting at the door, girl."

I laugh out loud. "He's not my boyfriend, Aunt Charlie. I just met him this evening."

"Well, I think he's a good boy, staying over here like that. You might wanna holla at him."

"Auntie!"

"I'm just sayin'."

I stretch again and walk over to Sam, who's leaning against the door with his eyes closed. He looks like he's asleep standing up.

"Sam, are you gonna be cool driving home?"

He opens his eyes. "I'm good. I was just resting my eyes."

"I think you should just stay here. It'll be okay if you sleep on one of the couches."

He smiles. "I'll be fine. But thanks for thinking 'bout me."

"You just make sure you call me when you get home."

Sam's smile widens. "Is that your sneaky way of trying to give me your phone number?"

"Boy, stop playing! I just want to make sure you get home okay."

"It's all right, Sunday. I like an aggressive woman. But all you had to do was give me your number. I would've taken it."

I roll my eyes and snatch Sam's phone to punch my number in. "Call me."

"What if I forget? Don't you want to have my number so you can check on me?"

I narrow my eyes and try to keep from smiling, but it's not working. I hand my phone to Sam. He glances at me with a mischievous smile as he punches the numbers in.

I'm totally enjoying this until I think about the fact that my mother is at the hospital with Carlos and he might not even make it through the night. How could I be out here laughing and joking when all this drama is taking place?

Sam hands my phone back to me and surprises me by giving me a hug. "It's gonna be all right. You know that, right?"

Okay, dang he smells good. And wow, I'm completely

attracted to him right now, even though he ain't the cutest dude. I mean, Romell's got him whipped in the looks department, but I know he'd never hug me and tell me everything's gonna be okay.

"I won't forget to call," Sam says, and then kisses me on my forehead before leaving.

I stand in the doorway and watch as he walks away. He stops to say something to Aunt Charlie and then gets into his car. I can't stop looking, even after he's driven up the hill and I can't even see his car anymore.

Okay . . . Romell who?

5

When I wake up in the morning, the first person I think about is Sam. He called me when he got in and told me to have sweet dreams. Is it selfish of me to be thinking of a potential crush when my mother's man is in the hospital? Maybe so, but I can't help it.

My mother is home now. She's sitting at the table holding on to a cup of coffee for dear life. She looks exhausted, but she still has on her clothes from yesterday.

"Mommy, what's the latest on Carlos?"

"No change. They say he could wake up at any time, or he might not. His family is up there with him."

"Why don't you get some rest? You look really tired."

"I am, but I'm more angry than tired."

"You're angry because Carlos got shot?"

She nods. "Definitely because of that, but even more because they robbed Carlos before the fight got started. It was all a setup to begin with."

"What? How do you know?"

My mother frowns. "That's why LaKeisha was up at the hospital apologizing. She told her brother that she was mad about Carlos being over here with me, and that she wanted to get him back for leaving her. They were never gonna let him be a part owner of the club."

I'm tripping that my mother is even telling me all this. She usually doesn't share "grown-folk business" with me and Dreya, but she's giving up all the dirt today.

"How much did they get him for?" I ask.

"Twenty-five thousand dollars."

"What? Where did Carlos get that kind of money?"

My mother's shoulders slump. "I loaned it to him. The club is already making lots of money, so it seemed like a sure thing. He was gonna give me double the money back."

"Mom, I didn't know you had money saved like that. I thought you only had my college fund and your retirement."

My mother is silent now as she sips on her coffee. Then it all comes to me. The reason why she's telling me all this, and where the twenty-five grand came from.

"You loaned him my college fund?" I ask.

She nods. "I promise, honey, I'm gonna find a way to get it back."

I think about the Spelman application that's on the desk in my bedroom. I plan to have it in by November 1st, so that I can get early admission. But how can I do that if I don't have money? I was already planning to apply for scholarships, too, but what if that doesn't pan out? What if I need more money?

The only thing that gets me through this hood existence sometimes is the fact that I'm going to college to get my law degree. When I study entertainment law, no slick producer or record company is gonna be able to scam me outta my royalties and residuals.

"I don't know what to say, Mommy. I'm going to college next year."

"Yes, you are. I don't even want you to worry about that. I'm gonna get the money. I just wanted you to know what was going on."

My mother and I look up when the front door opens. Dreya walks through the door looking rumpled, crumpled, and like she hasn't slept all night.

"You think you grown, staying out all night?" Aunt Charlie asks from her almost permanent spot on the couch. I thought she was still asleep.

Dreya gives Aunt Charlie the hand. "Don't stress me."

Aunt Charlie jumps up. "Don't stress you? You done lost your mind, I see! If you're that grown you can go stay with that boy. Go and pack yo' stuff!"

Dreya laughs and shakes her head. "How are you kicking me out of Aunt Shawn's house?"

Aunt Charlie looks at my mother, I guess trying to get some backup, but my mother throws both her hands up. "Unh-uh. I can't do it this morning, Charlie. That's between y'all."

"Oh, you ain't gon' back me up, Shawn? You ain't gon' put this triflin' heffa out?"

"Charlie . . ."

Aunt Charlie stands to her feet and her blanket drops to the floor, revealing a tattered nightgown and her ashy knees. It doesn't help that her legs are so skinny that they look like two pretzel sticks. Not a good look at all.

"Shawn! If Sunday was spending the night out with some thugged-out boy, I bet you wouldn't be so nonchalant."

My mother sighs and replies, "Charlie, I don't have the energy today."

Aunt Charlie looks my mother up and down. "I know I can't expect *you* to have my back. You done gave Sunday's college money to that ole wannabe thug, Carlos. If you'll do that to your own child, I know you wouldn't have *my* back."

"You need to go on somewhere with that, Charlie. If I didn't have your back, you and your children would be homeless. You betta recognize."

"See, why you gotta go there, Shawn?" Aunt Charlie asks.

My mother asks, "Why *you* gotta go there?"

I slide silently off the stool and flee to my bedroom. I can't even think about eating breakfast, 'cause my stomach is in knots. Even though my auntie and my mama's drama was a little bit of a distraction, I keep thinking about my college fund. I've been planning on going to Spelman since fifth grade, and as far as I know, my mother's been saving just as long.

After slamming my bedroom door hard, I throw myself onto my unmade bed and sob into my pillow. This is not fair at all.

"Sunday, unlock the door—I gotta change clothes!" Dreya hollers from the other side of the door.

I ignore her and stare at the ceiling. Even when Dreya starts pounding on the door and kicking it, I don't move. I don't feel like dealing with her right now.

The door rattles on its hinges as Dreya continues to kick like she ain't got good sense. I hope she kicks it in, so my mama can go upside her head. That would be exactly what I need to help get my mind off of this messed-up situation.

Finally, I walk over to the door and open it. Dreya acts like she's gonna swing on me and I don't even flinch. Actually, I almost laugh. Dreya going in on me is the last thing I'm worried about.

"Girl, please," I say, "I really wish you would. Today would be the perfect day for me to spank that—"

"Whatever, Sunday," Dreya interrupts. "If my man wasn't outside waiting on me, I'd wipe the floor with your lame self."

I chuckle. "Do it, Dreya. We can do this all day er'y day."

Dreya rolls her eyes and grabs her clothes. "Big D wants you to come to the studio."

She says this all nonchalantly, like it's nothing major.

"What for?" I ask, sounding pretty nonchalant myself. Don't want her to think I'm pressed.

"He wants to put together an album for me. He thinks he'll be able to blow me up when Truth's single hits the radio, just like Ashanti after she did them cuts for Big Pun and Ja Rule."

"What's in it for me?"

"A few stacks, I guess."

To make this worth my while, I'm gonna need way more than a few stacks. Even with scholarship money, I'm looking at a good thirty grand a year for school. And it sounds like my college fund is dang near depleted after operation Carlos.

"I don't know. I'll think about it."

"Big D said for you to call Sam and have him come scoop you. He told me to give you his number," Dreya says.

"I already have his number. Got it last night."

Dreya grins wickedly. "Got them digits, huh? Well, he's kinda your type, I guess, although he ain't nowhere near as cute as Romell."

"Who's thinkin' 'bout Romell?"

"You were up until five minutes ago!"

"Whatev."

Dreya rolls her eyes and grabs up a few more items and heads to the door. "Don't forget to call Sam, Sunday. This could really blow us up!"

As if she cares about blowing *us* up. She only cares about herself! I've never met anyone more out for themselves than Dreya.

When she leaves, I take out my phone and send Sam a text.

U gon' come scoop me?

It takes all of thirty seconds for him to respond. This makes me laugh out loud. Thirsty much?

U want me to?

I take a second to decide how I want this whole thing to play out. And since I don't know Sam all like that, I'm not gonna let him see me pressed.

Big D wants you to.

About a minute after I click Send, my phone rings. Guess who?

"Hey, Sam."

"So you don't want me to scoop you?"

I chuckle. "Didn't say that. But the text was a result of Big D's request."

"Okay. Well, then, yes, I'll come scoop you for Big D."

"Don't act like you don't want to."

"Didn't say that. But my scooping you is a result of Big D's request."

Wow. I'm speechless and caught without a comeback. Have I ever intellectually sparred with a guy before? I don't think so. This could be the start of something.

"How soon will you be here?"

"Does forty-five minutes work for you?" Sam asks. "I was kinda in the middle of something."

"Really? What are you in the middle of?"

"Hold on."

I can tell he puts the phone on speaker because I can hear shuffling going on in the background. The next thing I hear is music coming from a keyboard. It's a hot-sounding piano track. A simple melody weaved through a drum beat with the perfect amount of strings and horns. It's hot to death.

Sam says, "Did you hear that?"

"Yep. I like it."

"Good. Because Big D wants us to write something to this track for Dreya's album."

"Yeah, I haven't agreed to doing that yet. We're going to have to discuss the particulars. I'm not doing a whole album without songwriting credit."

"I hear you. I think he'll give you credit, but he'll just want his name on there first."

"You're cool with that? It seems kinda undignified."

"Well, you can choose to keep your dignity, or you can get your name out there. That's the way I look at it."

"I'll think about it while you're on your way to come and get me."

"Cool. Is everything okay with you?"

"Oh, you mean last night? Yeah, I guess. I'ma have to change some plans, but yeah, I'm good. See you in a little bit?"

"Not if I don't see you first."

I press End on my phone and I'm thinking how can this guy be so corny, yet likable at the same time?

6

"Fair exchange ain't robbery / but I feel like you robbin' me blind. / Losin' my mind, losin' myself / I write the lines while you stack the wealth."
—Sunday Tolliver

I'm bobbing my head to the track that Sam let me hear on the phone. We're holed up in a little room off the main studio. It's only a little bit bigger than a closet. The only thing in here is a keyboard, a few chairs, and a computer. Sam calls it his incubator because it's where his musical ideas come to life.

"You feeling anything?" Sam asks after playing the track all the way through.

I nod and sing, "I remember sweet things, like whispers in my ear / I love you was all I used to hear / But I pushed you away from me / 'Cause I was silly and I was not ready."

"That's hot!" Sam exclaims.

"You think so?"

Sam smiles and starts to play again. "Now I'm missing you / Wanna take back the way that I hurt you / But you ain't hearing me / 'Cause you found another one to re-place me."

"Dang, boy! You on fiyah!"

I try to hide my excitement just a little bit, but it's hard to contain with Sam feeding off me like this. I've never had a songwriting partner. It's always just been me. But Sam is the real deal.

Sam sits back in his chair and cheeses. "This song ought to be on your album. It's too hot to give to your cousin."

"My album? Nobody is trying to give me a record deal right now, but it's cool that you think I should be doing my own stuff."

"You're a much better singer than Dreya."

"Yeah, but you ought to see her perform. She's got stage presence like nobody's business."

Sam gives me a little frown. "I'm trying to compliment you, and you keep talking about your cousin."

"Well, we are working on songs for *her* album. She's about to be a star, not me."

"You're already a star."

I swallow hard and to keep from answering, I start singing again. "Love is / love does / love's gone / love was . . ."

"My eyes / can't hide / my tears / good-bye," Sam finishes.

We're silent now, just staring at each other in amazement. We just finished the first verse and hook of a song in less than an hour. It's mad hot, crazy hot.

"Whoa," Sam finally says.

"Yeah, I'm totally flatlined right now. I've never vibed with someone like this."

All of a sudden the air is thick, and I think I'm tripping. Sam looks away first, breaking the spell of our intense eye contact. Then the door to the room swings open, completely disintegrating our flow.

"Y'all coming up with anything?" Big D asks.

Sam looks at me and nods. He starts playing the track and I sing the first verse. Then Sam and I harmonize on the hook. It sounds sweet . . . and definitely too good for Dreya. But since nobody's checking for the next Sunday Tolliver joint, it's gonna have to go to Dreya.

"Dang! If I leave y'all in here all day, we gon' go platinum, no question!" Big D exclaims. "This the bidness, for real."

Sam smiles. "She's good, Big D. Like a muse or something."

"Stop playing, boy," I say, while I'm totally blushing. "You're good, too."

"Hey! No crushing and whatnot in my lab!" Big D says. "This here is about the paper, know what I mean?"

"Yeah, Big D, we hear you," Sam chuckles.

Big D stares me down. "I hear you want some song-writer credit, lil' mama."

"Yeah, no doubt."

I'm trying to sound cool, but I don't feel cool at all. I feel like Eminem in that movie *8 Mile* and this is like my one shot to blow up. I cannot mess this up. Everything's riding on this. College, my career. It's do-or-die time.

"Your name can go behind mine and Sam's on the

track listing. You'll get a flat fee of one thousand per song."

"One thousand? What if it goes platinum?"

Big D shrugs. "What if it doesn't?"

"So I write ten songs and make ten thousand dollars. That doesn't seem like a lot. What if I just wait and get my money on the back end?"

Sam's eyebrows rise as if I've said too much, but Big D looks like he's contemplating what I'm saying.

"Tell you what—ten thousand on the first time out, and if this goes platinum, you're in a good position for the sophomore album."

I consider my options. Ten thousand dollars is a lot of money. At least I know I'll be able to start my freshman year at Spelman. But I'll be sick to death if Dreya's album goes platinum, which I know it will, and Big D makes millions while I'm still struggling.

Dreya sticks her head in the door. "Girl, who else is paying you a thousand dollars a song?"

"It just feels like I'm getting played," I say.

Big D replies, "Listen, you don't get to start out on top, baby. You got to work your way up. Most cats out here on the come-up would write songs for me, for free. I'm paying you because I know you got what it takes to go the distance. But you got to crawl before you walk, baby."

I take in a deep breath and let it out slowly. "Okay. I'll do it."

Sam exhales like he's relieved. But he's probably got something riding on this, too. Something tells me I should've gotten a lawyer.

But that's not how deals go down in the A.

"It's a wrap, then," Big D says. "I'ma let y'all get back to work. Make it hot."

When Big D and Dreya leave the room, Sam says, "You cool?"

"I guess. I feel like I just sold my soul."

"Don't think about it like that. We are about to blow up, Sunday."

"But only Big D is gonna get paid?"

Sam shakes his head. "We will, too. As soon as Dreya gets a number-one hit, everybody will want us to write for them."

"Mmm-hmm . . ."

"Trust me, girl. I know what I'm talking about."

I guess I do have to trust him and Big D. What other choice do I have? I know one thing, though. Dreya better step up to the plate and sing like my college dreams depend on it.

7

Getting dressed for school this morning is tough. I spent all day Saturday and Sunday creating and vibing with Sam in the think tank. We came up with not ten, but twelve hot songs, and I'm dog tired.

I go to my purse and pull out the check. It doesn't even seem real that I'm holding a ten-thousand-dollar check in my hand. I'm going on my lunch to open a bank account at the Bank of America across the street from my school.

Dreya stands looking in the mirror, trying to perfect her hobo-couture look. "We're about to get paid, Sunday."

"Do you really believe all that stuff Big D is talking? Platinum sales, millions of dollars, and all that?"

"Yeah. He's gonna make me a star, for real. That's why I'm moving out today. I'm moving into Big D's house."

"What? Auntie Charlie isn't gonna let you do that."

"She can't stop me. Plus, as soon as I get a record deal, she'll change her tune. She's all about the paper."

"Are you packing anything, or are you just gonna leave?"

Dreya rolls her eyes. "Girl, you know if I pack up and try to have an official move, it's gonna be a hot, drama-filled mess."

"So you're just gonna go with nothing?"

"Truth said he'd take me shopping and buy me all new clothes. I'll need them anyway, because I have to go with him to all his release parties and performances."

"And his album comes out when?"

"End of November, but we're about to start promoting it now."

All of this is happening too fast. Dreya's moving in with Big D, promoting an album, and recording her own. I'm holding a ten-thousand-dollar check in my hands.

"What about school?" I ask, thinking that I might already know the answer.

Dreya laughs. "Sunday, you're the bookworm of the family. I wasn't ever college-bound, know what I mean?"

"I guess, but I don't think you should move out yet."

"Are you hating on me, Sunday? You trying to hold me back 'cause you don't have a man like Truth, or a record deal?"

"Girl, please. You ain't even got a record deal yet. This just all sounds too good to be true."

"And what about that check in your hand? Is that too good to be true, too?"

"It is if it bounces."

Dreya laughs again and this time grabs up her leather backpack. "I'm out. Don't tell my mother about me moving."

I follow Dreya up to the front of the house, where Aunt Charlie is watching a Will Smith movie and smoking a cigarette. Can we watch the news in the morning like normal people, please?

"Where y'all been all weekend?" Aunt Charlie asks.

"The studio," I reply.

"Well, I hope you got your homework done," my mother comments.

"Why do you care if I did my homework? You up here spending all of my college money, so I might as well drop out, right?"

My mother sighs wearily. "How many times do I have to apologize to you, Sunday? Plus, I told you we're getting the money back. As soon as Carlos is back on his feet—"

"*If* Carlos ever gets back on his feet," Aunt Charlie says.

"He's going to, Charlie," my mother snaps. "Why would you even go there?"

I decide not to comment on Aunt Charlie's ignorance. I do hope that Carlos gets well, but what's the point of talking about it? It looks like Big D is funding my college education now.

Both Dreya and I leave the house. Truth's car is waiting outside for Dreya, and Bethany is standing in front of our house with an impatient look on her face.

Bethany says, "It's about time. You're gonna make us miss the bus."

"We got plenty of time, girl. Come on."

As we walk, Bethany asks, "Is it true what I heard about Carlos?"

"I don't know. I guess."

"That's messed up. The whole neighborhood is talking about it."

This means that Bethany spent the weekend at the mall and at Cascade skating rink telling everybody my business.

When we get to the bus stop, my ex-boo Romell steps up to me, with his boys following close behind. I can tell by that slick grin on his face that he's got something ignorant to say.

I am definitely not in the mood.

"I heard your mama's man got shot up. Who'd he do dirty?" Romell asks.

Ugh! I can't believe I used to be so gone over this boy. Sam only knew me for one day and cared more than Romell does.

"I don't know, why don't you ask him?" I reply with the stank attitude dripping from my tone.

"Dang, Sunday. Why you gotta be all like that? See, that's why I had to bounce your little evil self to the curb," Romell says.

"You did not kick me to the curb. I bounced you."

"That's right. You were mad, just 'cause I gave some other girl my number. Are you still mad?"

"Naw. I'm mad 'cause you up in my face and your breath stank. Bethany, give him some gum, a mint, something."

Everyone at the bus stop cracks up laughing. I lift one

eyebrow, challenging Romell to come at me again. He will never beat me in a war of words, but it might make me feel better.

I guess Romell doesn't want to take the chance of me embarrassing him further, so he gives me a dismissive shrug and walks off with his boys to the other side of the bus stop.

"So y'all were at the studio all weekend?" Bethany asks. "Are you gonna dish or what?"

"Nothing to dish about."

"Why didn't you come and get me?"

"I don't know. It was kinda last minute. Big D wanted me to come into the studio and write some songs for Dreya's album."

Bethany's mouth drops open. "Dreya's album? Y'all tripping not keeping me in the loop. She's got a record deal?"

"Not yet, but Big D said he could get her one as soon as Truth's first single hits number one. Maybe even before that."

"The hook we wrote?" Bethany asks.

I laugh out loud. "Stop playing, Bethany. The hook I wrote?"

"Yeah, it's whatever. I contributed, too," she says.

"Okay, Bethany." I refuse to argue with her when she's being delusional.

"What's up with Sam? You aren't trying to step to him, are you?"

I pause before giving my reply. I know that Bethany likes Sam, or thinks she likes Sam, or whatever it is that she does. In her mind she's claimed him, but nobody else operates off her logic.

Finally I say, "He's a great songwriter, but I don't know about stepping to him. We just met."

Bethany rolls her neck and leans back. Here we go. Let the delusional behavior begin.

"Is that the *only* reason you're not stepping to him?" she asks.

"Yeah, pretty much."

"How about the fact that I was digging him first?"

See what I'm talking about? Delusional.

"Bethany, don't start. Sam was not feeling you at all, and you know it. Why you always gotta do this?"

This is such a repeat story with Bethany. Just about every guy that I've dated, including Romell, has caused drama between us. And it's the same story every time. She saw the guy first, and I stole him. Then she has an attitude until she finds some other guy to like. It's old, for real. I really wish she'd change the channel on that stupidity.

"I'm not pressed about it," Bethany retorts. "I just wanted you to know that I saw Sam first. He's not even cute, so you can have him."

"Bethany, we all met him at the same time, but whatever. I don't even care what you think."

"Yeah, it *is* whatever."

Bethany crosses her arms and slumps back in the seat. This is the part where she decides she's not talking to me for all of like five minutes. This is so repetitive, like my iPod stuck on replay.

"Are you going to the studio again after school?" Bethany asks. I guess the silent treatment is over. What was that, thirty seconds?

I nod. "Yep. Dreya is set to start recording. Sam is coming to pick me up."

"Is it cool if I come, too?"

"Not if you're gonna be tripping and embarrassing me."

Bethany sucks her teeth and pouts. "Now you sound like Dreya."

"I'm just saying."

"Don't be acting like I'm not a part of this group, Sunday. I've been in Daddy's Little Girls since day one." Bethany's voice quivers as she says this, as if she's really afraid that we're going to leave her behind.

"I know, girl. If one of us comes up, you know it's gonna be all of us."

I hear the words come out of my mouth, but I wonder . . . are we all gonna come up? Or is it just going to be Dreya? Maybe the group should've been called Daddy's Little Girl.

Later, in English class, my friend Margit pounces on me as soon as she sees me. "Are you all right?" she asks.

"Yes . . ."

"I heard about the shooting at your house, and I was just making sure you didn't get caught by a stray bullet. Was it a drive-by?"

"I don't think so. This isn't Compton, Margit."

"Well, I'm just saying. Bethany was at Cascade telling everybody about it."

I knew it! Big-mouth heffa!

"And you wanna know what else she was doing?"

"What?"

"Well, you didn't hear it from me, but she was all up on Romell during the couple skate, grinding and stuff!"

I give a nonchalant shrug. "I don't care about that. Romell is yesterday's news."

"I know," Margit replies. "I just thought it was kinda twisted."

I'm glad that class starts because I'm ready to end this conversation with Margit. If I were still up on Romell, I'd be mad, but it's whatever. Bethany's thirsty self can have him, because I'm about to do the dang thing and get this music thing on lock.

8

By the time Sam gets me and Bethany to the studio, Dreya's already been recording for hours. She didn't come to school today, so I guess she's made her choice. Giving up on school for the fab life. I can't get with that, but I'm not Dreya.

Truth is chilling in the studio lounge, eating a plate of fried chicken, macaroni and cheese, and collard greens. There's also a glass of what looks like cherry Kool-Aid on the coffee table in front of him. He looks up at us and grins.

"What took y'all so long? Shelly been burning it up in the kitchen, fryin' chicken like she Martha Stewart or somebody."

Bethany asks, "What makes you think Martha Stewart can make good fried chicken? She ain't even from down South."

My stomach growls, and I grab it in embarrassment. "Sorry, y'all. I had an early lunch."

"It's cool, shortie. You want me to fix you a plate?" Truth asks.

"You gon' fix me a plate?" I stare at him in disbelief. Truth doesn't seem like the type to wait on anybody, much less a girl.

He laughs out loud. "Sam, can you tell this girl? I'm a gentleman. You want something, too, Bethany?"

"I sure do," Bethany says, "and don't be stingy on that mac and cheese. It looks like it's slammin'."

"It is. Shelly can cook her butt off, and with the size of her booty, that's pretty good."

Now it's my turn to laugh. I've never seen this side of Truth before. It almost makes his ole gremlin-lookin' tatted-up self a little bit cute.

"I'll help you," I say. "You can't carry everybody's food. You want something, Sam?"

Sam gives me a bright smile. "You fixing my food now? That is so sweet."

"Boy . . ."

"All right, all right. I'll take some chicken and greens. No mac and cheese, though. It'll make me want to take a nap."

I follow Truth into the kitchen. He washes and dries his hands in the sink and reaches for plates.

"I won't tell your boys how domesticated you are," I say with a giggle.

"Domesticated, huh? Nah, never that. I'm just taking care of y'all, 'cause y'all Big D's guests. It's called hospitality."

For some reason this reminds me of a scene out of that old-school movie *The Godfather*. All the gangsters and killers are sitting in a kitchen while this big, fat, thugged-out dude makes a pot of spaghetti. Like for real, gangsters gotta eat, too.

"It's cool. It's actually a good look for you," I comment. "You can't be thugged out twenty-four seven."

Truth grins at me and hands me a plate. "You don't like thugs? I thought all y'all liked thugs."

"I like for-real people, so if you're really a thug, do you."

"Dreya never told me how cool you are, Sunday. I feel bad now for letting you walk to the bus stop all those times. I coulda dropped you off."

"It's all good. Me and Bethany weren't trying to interfere in y'all little morning dates or whatever."

Truth licks his lips and looks me up and down in a way that makes me totally uncomfortable. I'm not one for doing anything shady with my cousin's boyfriend. I don't roll like that.

"You and Sam did y'all thing on Dreya's album tracks," Truth says as he finishes making the second plate.

"Thanks. Sam is really good and we're on the same page. That's pretty rare, so I'm glad we found each other."

Truth replies, "Found each other? Sounds kinda romantic. I thought you were talking about writing songs."

"You sound jealous."

Truth chuckles. "Nah, not jealous. I can have any chick I want—even you."

This dude is beyond cocky, I guess because he's about to blow up in the rap game. And I guess he is kinda built. He's got muscle tone that won't quit, and the black tank top he's wearing isn't hiding any of it.

But none of that makes me wanna holla at him, because all that thuggishness cancels the good stuff out. I'd take a chill dude like Sam any day. Sam's swagger isn't oozing from his pores, but it's there.

I take the other plate from Truth. "Thanks for the grub."

"So you just gon' leave me by myself, making the last plate?" he asks.

"Pretty much. Your ego can keep you company."

I hear Truth laughing as I turn my back on him and walk away. Dude has left a bad taste in my mouth.

When I get back to the lounge with the plates, Sam and Bethany are both sitting on the couch. Dreya is up here, too, fanning herself and swigging off a bottle of water. I pause because I'm not sure where to sit down. Bethany knows that something might be up with me and Sam, so she should've sat on the other couch or chair, because there is not enough room for me on the couch with her and Sam.

I hand Sam his plate. "This enough for you?"

"Yes. Thanks, Sunday."

Dreya's eyes dart around the room. "Where is Truth?"

"In the kitchen fixing my food," Bethany says.

"What?" Dreya asks. She closes her eyes like she's trying to contain herself. "Bethany, you better be glad I have to preserve my voice, or I'd be cussing your big butt out right now."

Dreya storms down the hall toward the kitchen and I give Bethany the serious eye.

"You're dead wrong for that," Sam says.

"What?" Bethany gives both of us her fake innocent gaze.

Before I get a chance to chime in, we hear some kind of pandemonium going on in the kitchen. Sounds like plates and glasses breaking. I guess Dreya's in there regulating.

"Are you gonna see what's up or am I?" Sam asks me.

I put both my hands up and shake my head. "Not me. I don't do drama."

But neither of us have to go, because Truth and Dreya both come back into the room. Dreya's face is about three shades of evil, and I'm not surprised that Truth is not holding a plate of food for Bethany. From all the commotion I heard, I thought that Truth would be wearing that plate of food.

"If you want something to eat, go and get it yourself," Dreya tells Bethany in a quiet voice. "My man don't fix plates for nobody."

Ha! She's only quiet because she's still got singing to do this evening. She would so be hollering right now if that wasn't the case.

Big D comes up the steps and into the lounge. He's got a really intense frown on his face. I'm glad he's looking in Dreya's and Truth's direction with that mean mug, and not mine.

"Dreya, you need to get down here and finish recording this song."

"I came up here to get some water, and then I had to end up handling something," Dreya replies.

Big D says, "Sweetheart, I'm not on this today. I just got off the phone with Epsilon Records and they liked the singles I sent them with your vocals. They wanna offer you a deal and you up here on some drama."

"Epsilon Records wants to offer me a deal? But Truth's single isn't even out yet." Dreya's hands are trembling so hard that I can feel her excitement from where I'm sitting.

"That's how it works sometimes," Big D says. "The industry is unpredictable."

"She's *always* on some drama," Bethany says.

Sam swallows a bite of food and interjects. "Actually, that might be a good stage name for you, Dreya. You should call yourself Drama."

Truth gives Sam a fist pound. "That's wassup, dog! The only way you gon' blow up is to get the bloggers and paparazzi all up in your bidness. With a name like Drama, you just givin' 'em an invitation."

Dreya still looks like she's not really feeling the idea, although I think it's a good one. We're in the A, land of the black celebrities and the bloggers who love to stalk them. We got T.I., Tiny, Janet, Jermaine, Usher, and the *Real Housewives*. Shoot, last I heard we had little Rudy Huxtable, all grown up and kickin' it diva-style.

Big D says, "I'm diggin' this. One-name R & B stars are hot right now. What you think, Drama?"

Dreya's head snaps up and she strikes a divalicious pose. "Huh? Do I know you?"

Everybody bursts into laughter. Yeah, being a diva is definitely something Dreya can pull off. It's how she is all day everyday anyway. Now she just has a record deal to go along with it.

"So, Big D," Bethany asks, "are Sunday and I singing backup vocals on Dreya's album?"

Big D shakes his head. "Nah, we got it covered. Dreya is gonna sing her own backup vocals."

"Yeah, Bethany," Dreya says. "I don't need you down there trying to hit some Mariah Carey high notes on my track."

Bethany frowns and rolls her eyes at Dreya. I know what she's thinking, because I'm pretty much thinking the same thing. She owes all of this to Daddy's Little Girls, including having Truth as a boyfriend and the record deal.

"I can't believe you're trying to trip and leave Daddy's Little Girls in the dust. Don't you remember how you even met Truth?" I ask Dreya.

"Yeah, and . . . ?"

We were in a local talent search and Truth was one of the judges. Even though I was singing lead, Dreya's dropping down and sweeping the floor with it was what got us second prize. We got to meet Truth as part of our prize, and he started digging her.

Truth chuckles. "Yeah, I remember that, Sunday. You were singing your butt off, wasn't you, ma?"

"Yeah, I was, and so was Bethany. Dreya did a lot of dancing, though."

"I was singing, too," Dreya argues. "And I'm the reason why we won! I got the crowd pumped."

I say, "That might be true, but you wouldn't have been in the show if it wasn't for our group. Now you trying to dis us?"

I can feel my attitude rising up for real now. It's making this macaroni and cheese bubble up in my stomach. Maybe I'm just stressed about my college fund going up in smoke. Or maybe I'm tripping because this should be my big break and not old, ungrateful Dreya's.

"It's just the business," Big D replies. "Sometimes you make it as a group, and sometimes one person has to get on and bring everybody else on later. It's still love, though."

"Right," Dreya says. "It's still love. Someday, I'ma be able to help y'all blow up, too."

Is it just me, or is Dreya getting ahead of herself? She hasn't even signed the record deal yet, but now she's gonna help me and Bethany blow up? Really?

"Come on, Ms. Drama," Big D says. "We've got an album to finish recording."

"I think my voice needs a rest, Big D. My throat hurts. Can we finish tomorrow?"

"Shelly!" Big D calls down the stairs. "Can you fix Dreya some tea? We need her to belt out one more song tonight. I've got a meeting with Epsilon's head A&R rep in the morning."

Shelly sashays up the stairs slowly. She sure likes to keep her store-bought body on display. She's wearing leggings that I'm pretty sure were meant to go under something, but she's paired them with a tiny baby tee that leaves nothing to the imagination.

"Okay, baby," Shelly replies. "What kind of tea you like, Dreya? We've got peppermint and peach."

Dreya frowns. "Neither one of them sounds good."

Shelly lifts an eyebrow and gives Dreya a blank stare. "Big D says you're drinking tea, so I suggest you pick one."

Sufficiently checked, Dreya replies in a tiny voice, "Peach."

"Come on back downstairs while Shelly hooks that up," Big D says. "I want you to listen to what you've laid down so far and think about where you wanna put in some runs."

"Make sure she doesn't go flat when she does a run," I say to Big D. "She does that a lot. The entire run will be sweet until the last note."

Big D turns his attention back to Dreya. "Give me a run."

Dreya closes her eyes and sings the alphabet song. Yeah, A, B, C, D, etc. We had this version of it that we used to harmonize on for warm-ups. Dreya goes up a few notes and hits a run on the way down and the end of it is a mess.

"See what I mean?" I ask.

"Shut up, Sunday," Dreya says.

"Let me hear you do it, Sunday," Big D says. "I've got an idea."

I do the same melody as Dreya, but I choose a different point in the tune to do my run. Of course it's flawless. What can I say? Singing comes naturally to me.

Big D looks like the wheels in his brain are turning. "I take back what I said about y'all singing on Dreya's album."

"You're gonna let us sing backup?" Bethany squeals.

"No, but I'm gonna have Sam do his studio magic and layer Sunday's vocals under Dreya's. You think it'll work, Sam?"

Sam nods. "They have very similar-sounding voices,

but Sunday will have to pull back a little bit. Her vocals are too strong; they'll overpower Dreya's. Then everyone will trip if they hear Dreya singing live and she doesn't sound anything like the recording."

"Her voice won't hardly overpower mine. You don't know what you're talking about, Sam!" Dreya fusses.

Sam is silent now. He pops his last bite of food into his mouth and sets his plate down on the table.

"Well, nobody really expects an artist to sound the same live as they do on the recording," Bethany says in a very small, quiet voice.

Big D replies, "Exactly. So, Sam, make it do what it do. Get Sunday in the sound booth."

"Is anybody gonna ask me how I feel about this?" I ask.

"What's not to like?" Big D asks. "But I know what you're thinking."

"You do?"

"Yes, you're thinking that you need some additional compensation to do the background vocals."

I give Big D a tiny smile. "I'm glad we're on the same page."

9

"**Y**ou rocked those background vocals, Sunday. If Dreya gets a record deal, she'll have you to thank," Sam says.

He's driving me home from the studio. It would've been me and Bethany, but she got heated about me singing on the CD and her vocals not being required. She called some dude from school to come and pick her up, and left while I was still recording.

"Thanks. It blows that she's gonna get a record deal, though, while I'm still on the come-up."

"Yeah, but who knows? Yours could be coming sooner than you think."

"What makes you think that?" I ask.

"Got a feeling, I guess."

I think about going home and hearing about the latest update on Carlos, and get bummed all over again. A lot of good Sam's feeling is gonna do me when it's time to pay my tuition at Spelman. The thought of community college or no college at all makes me let out a long sigh.

"What you thinkin' about?" Sam asks.

"Nothing."

I'm not ready to have Sam all up in my business yet, no matter how cool he seems. He already knows too much, from the one time he dropped me off.

"Okay, I get it. I don't know you like that to get all up in your mix, right?"

"Pretty much."

"So what if I say I want to get to know you better?" he asks.

"You are getting to know me better. You definitely know more about me today than you knew on the first day we met."

Sam laughs out loud. "Do you always make guys work this hard, or are you just giving that to me?"

"My mama told me that you appreciate something more if you have to work for it."

Sam smiles but doesn't reply. He keeps his eyes on the road as he slows on the freeway and takes my exit on I-20.

I say, "That was a good idea you had about Dreya having a stage name."

"Yeah, her real name isn't all that memorable."

"But no one will forget a singer named Drama," I concur.

"And soon people will be singing her songs. Or should I say *our* songs?"

"I'd like it better if you said *our* songs."

Sam lifts his eyebrows and smiles. "Okay, our songs then. Do you want me to walk you in?"

I peer out the window, and everything looks pretty calm at my house. No police cars or any other evidence of drama, but still I don't think it's a good idea to have Sam walk me in. There's no telling what Aunt Charlie is wearing! And, of course, whatever crazy ensemble she's sporting is gonna be on display for everyone to see, from her post on the living room couch.

"You don't have to walk me in, Sam. I'm a big girl."

He laughs. "Still playing hard."

"'Bye, Sam. Will you need me at the studio tomorrow?"

"No, I don't think so. The recording is complete, but I'll have to mix and master everything."

I have no idea what mix and master means, but I suspect it's something technical that they do to make everything sound extra hot.

Sam puts his car in park, like he's in no hurry to leave, even though I've opened the door on my side. I surprise myself by wondering when I'm going to see Sam again after tonight, since I won't have to go to the studio anytime soon.

"Are you sure you don't want to kick it with me?" Sam asks.

"Kick it with you where?"

"Dinner and a movie? Bowling? Shoot, I don't know."

"You don't know."

Sam sighs. "I just know I wanna spend some time with you."

"I'll think about it. Just don't lose my number."

"All right, toughie, I won't."

I get out of the car and start up the driveway, but not

without checking over my shoulder to see if Sam is watching. He is.

As soon as I open the door to our house, I can tell that something is not right. My mother is putting on her coat, and Aunt Charlie is pacing the floor.

"What's wrong?" I ask.

"It's Carlos," my mother says. "He's disappeared from the hospital. The police want me to come down there. . . ."

"Disappeared? I thought he was unconscious or something! How has he disappeared?" I ask.

"I don't know, and the police don't, either. His mother and sister are not talking, so I think they might know where he is or have something to do with it."

I cover my mouth with my hand. "Do you think he's hiding out somewhere?"

"I don't know," my mother says as tears rush down her face. "Maybe he is, or maybe those thugs from the club came to finish off the job."

My mom rushes out the door, but Aunt Charlie keeps pacing the floor. She and Carlos weren't all that tight, so I don't understand why she's so worried.

"Aunt Charlie, Carlos is gonna be okay."

She gives me a strange look and asks, "Sunday, where is Dreya? I been calling her cell phone and she's not picking up."

"She didn't tell you where she was going?" I ask. "She's at the studio, I guess. She's probably staying there."

Aunt Charlie cocks her head to one side as if she's pondering what I'm saying. "What do you mean, she's staying there? She don't think she's got to come home?"

"I don't know what she thinks," I say with a shrug. "I just left her, and she didn't seem in a hurry."

"Call her for me on your phone," Aunt Charlie says.

"Unh-uh. This is between y'all. If she won't answer her phone . . ."

Aunt Charlie jumps up so fast, she looks like a blur. Next thing I know she's in my face, and I can literally taste the smoke she blows out of her nose. Ugh.

"I ain't playing with you, Sunday. Call your cousin."

I roll my eyes at Aunt Charlie as I punch in Dreya's number. I hold the phone up to my face as it rings, but as soon as I get the first syllable of "hello" out of my mouth, Aunt Charlie snatches my phone.

"Dreya, where are you?" Aunt Charlie asks.

"What do you mean, you ain't coming home?" Aunt Charlie screams into my phone.

I'm gonna need a wet wipe and some hand sanitizer to get all her spit, cigarette ashes, and bacteria off my phone.

"I don't care about no record deal, and I ain't heard of nobody named Big D. I'm gonna send the police after your behind."

I plop down in my mother's beanbag chair to wait for my phone. I knew I shouldn't have let Aunt Charlie use my phone to call Dreya. This might take all night.

"She hung up on me," Aunt Charlie says with a look of surprise on her face.

"Can I have my phone back now?"

Aunt Charlie tosses the phone over to me. "What is she talking about—a record deal, Sunday? Is this legit? Has she signed anything yet?"

"Big D seems legit to me. Truth's record is about to come out next month."

"This is your fault, Sunday. All that singing group mess, and now my daughter is living with some man, talking about a record deal."

"How is it my fault? I'm not living over some dude's house. You trippin', Aunt Charlie."

I pull myself up from the beanbag chair and stomp all the way to my bedroom. Me storming off to my room is getting to be a regular thing.

I lie across my bed and open my backpack. Dreya might've quit school for her record deal, but I've still got homework. Ugh, calculus. This is the one subject I could've bypassed because, for real, how many entertainment lawyers have to know anything about derivatives and differential equations?

When I'm about halfway through the exercises, my phone rings. I hesitate before answering because it's Romell's ringtone. I don't know if I feel like verbally sparring with him right now. And why does he even still have his own ringtone? I need to dead that, for real.

"What's up, Romell?" I ask, wanting him to get right into the conversation.

"How you been, Sunday? You haven't called or texted me in a minute."

"We broke up, remember?"

"Yeah, I thought we were gonna get back together, though."

Something about this conversation doesn't sound right. First of all, we have never talked about getting back together. Second, Romell is never this nice. I can't ever remember him just calling to ask how I'm doing. He does not roll like that.

"Romell, what's up? I'm doing some homework, so could you hurry up and get to the point?"

"Why you gotta be like that?"

I let out a loud sigh. "What is it, Romell?"

"I just heard your cousin singing on the Internet," he says.

"Seriously? What's the name of the song?" I ask, hoping that it's none of my stuff that's leaked.

"She's just singing the hook. It's some new rapper dude. 'What Ya Gonna Do,' or something like that."

"Wow, for real? Did you like the song?"

"It was fiyah!" Romell says. "Dreya's 'bout to blow up."

"How do you know it's her?"

"Somebody posted the link on Facebook and said it was her."

"What Web site is it on?"

"Mediatakeout.com."

"Thanks. Lemme call you back, okay?"

After I press End on my phone, I boot up my slow, raggedy desktop computer and hope I can get a good Internet connection. While I'm waiting for it to come on, I dial Sam's number.

"Hey, Sunday. I didn't think you'd miss me this soon."

I crack up laughing. "Sam, you are silly. I don't miss you, boy."

"Sure you don't. What's up?"

"This boy from school called and told me that he heard Dreya singing on the Internet."

"Yeah, I know."

"You know and you didn't tell me? That's my work out there on the Internet being listened to for free!"

"Calm down, calm down. Big D leaked the track himself—it's cool."

Okay, now I'm confused.

"Why would Big D leak his own track?" I ask.

"Publicity. Nobody really knew who Truth was, outside of Atlanta and a few underground circuits in New York. Now teenagers all over the country are bobbing their heads to your hook, girl. You should be happy!"

"I should be happy?"

"Yeah, toughie. Your cousin's life is about to change."

Everybody keeps telling me about Dreya's life changing. Well, mine has been changing, too, and not all for the better. How can I get excited about kids loving the track when nobody even knows that I wrote it?

Sam asks, "You okay, Sunday? You don't sound pumped about all this."

"I guess I'm still trying to get used to the idea of Dreya's name being up in lights."

"I've got a feeling yours will be, too."

"I don't even care about all that. I just want to go to college like a normal teenager."

Sam laughs out loud. "Normal? After Drama's album comes out, our lives will never be normal again."

10

Dreya decides to show up at school the day after the track leaks. Me and Bethany are standing next to my locker and watching Dreya's Academy Award–worthy performance. She's even carrying a leather backpack! I wonder what's in there, because we all know it's not books. Usually it's clothes for when she spends the night over at her boyfriend's house. But since she lives over at Big D's now, that's not necessary.

She struts up the hallway and leans against the lockers across from us as if she's waiting for the paparazzi to come and the cameras to start flashing. She's got the diva pose down pat, too. Utter hilarity. I wonder if she watched a bunch of Rihanna footage for her diva education.

My ex-boo, Romell, is the main one heading up the Dreya fan club. I kind of find that hard to believe, since he's never been checking for Dreya before, but I guess a hot track can change a lot of things. In my eyes, his Dreya-jocking takes his swagger levels into the negative numbers.

Romell and a small crowd of people surround Dreya. Of course, Bethany and I want to hear what she's gonna say, so we've got to join the crowd. I don't like feeling like one of Dreya's groupies, especially since Sam and I wrote all her songs.

"So, Dreya, you got a record deal?" Romell asks.

"My lawyers told me that I'm not allowed to talk about it," she replies.

Bethany covers her mouth and chuckles. "What lawyers?" she whispers to me.

"Girl, I don't know."

"And does she even have the record deal yet?"

I shrug. "Last I heard, Big D was trying to make it happen. Maybe something's changed since yesterday."

"Do you think she's gonna tell anyone that you wrote that hook?"

Now it's my turn to laugh. "We're talking about Dreya, Bethany. You and I both know she's not giving me credit for anything."

Why are people turned around looking at me and Bethany like we're being rude? It's not like Dreya's saying anything important. She's not a celebrity yet! And even if she does reach celeb status, it's not going to make her mindless ramblings any smarter.

Do I sound like a hater right now? Well, it's whatever. Call me a hater with a capital *H* then.

"I can't tell you about a record deal, but that single y'all heard drops the week of Thanksgiving. It's called

'What Ya Gonna Do.' Y'all really need to cop that ring-tone and MP3."

Is this chick marketing now? Wow. I've never seen Dreya work hard doing anything; she's pretty much a bump effort kinda girl. It's even funnier because she's not going to make any money off the track, although it will definitely help her popularity if it goes to number one on the charts.

"I heard on the radio that Truth was going on a pro-motional tour," Romell says. "Are you going with him?"

"You know it!" Dreya says. "We're going to ten cities, doing shows. It's gonna be fiyah, for real."

She's going on tour now? Talk about being out of the loop. Is this what Sam was talking about when he said Dreya's life was about to change?

I'm trying not to feel jealous, but I can't help it. She's so mean and spiteful. Why should she be the one to blow up? I could sure use some record-deal money myself, 'cause Spelman ain't free.

Speaking of Spelman, I need to get myself to class, be-cause I've got a calculus test this morning.

"I've got to go to class," I say to Bethany. "I'll see you later."

"Okay. You gonna be in the cafeteria at lunchtime?" she asks.

I nod. "Yeah. Holla."

That test was ridiculous. I'm glad I took some time to do my homework, 'cause I wouldn't have passed it if I hadn't. But at least it's over, and the rest of my morning classes were cake.

I scan the cafeteria for Bethany, but I guess she's not here yet, because I can't find her. But guess who I do see? Ms. Dreya—oops, Drama—and her man, Truth, sitting on a table with a small crowd surrounding them. I wonder how Truth got past the security guards. He's our age, but he definitely doesn't go to school here or anywhere else.

I pretend that I don't see them, because I'm sooo not joining the groupie crowd this afternoon. The whole morning performance gave me an upset stomach.

Finally Bethany walks up, and she's practically beaming. About what I have no idea, but the girl is grinning from ear to ear.

"What are you cheesing about?" I ask.

"Jordan asked me to go to prom with him."

"Seriously? It's only October twentieth! Prom is months away."

"You better hurry and find a date, Sunday. After winter break, everybody good will be taken and you'll end up with somebody from the geek squad."

"I'm not finding a date. A date better find me. I don't chase boys—you know that, Bethany."

She narrows her eyes. "Right, you just steal them from your best friend."

"You're back on that?"

"I never really got off of it, Sunday. Last year it was Romell, now it's Sam. But it's all good, because me and Jordan are together now."

"Yay, you."

"Is that Truth over there with Dreya? What's he doing here?"

"My first guess is that he's doing promo work for the single."

"Let's go over there."

"You can if you want, but I'm cool."

Bethany shrugs and walks over to the crowd, confirming her groupie status. No, thank you.

Truth spots me and waves for me to come over. I hesitate, thinking about his flirting with me at the studio. I'm not trying to get all close to him, because that seems like a hot mess waiting to happen.

But because he keeps waving me over, now everyone in their groupie circle is staring at me. It looks like I don't have any choice but to go over there and hang. This is most definitely against my better judgment.

As I walk up to the table, Truth blurts, "Y'all know Sunday, right? She be dropping them hot lyrics and hooks. She wrote the hook for 'What Ya Gonna Do.' "

Dreya looks hotter than buffalo wings with fire sauce. I'm confused and totally shocked that Truth gave me credit like he did, especially since my name probably won't show up anywhere on the track listing.

I give the new Dreya fan club a tiny nod and escape to the lunch line. Yeah, I know I completely spazzed, but Truth didn't leave me much choice. What was I supposed to do? Slide on the table next to Truth and make him a Tolliver sandwich?

Nah, that would not have gone down without foolishness popping off. Most likely, Dreya would've been the cause of it.

Bethany catches up with me in the lunch line. "What was up with the Truth shout-out?"

"I have no idea."

"Umph, umph, umph," Bethany says, sounding like my grandmother when she's heard some gossip about one of her church friends.

"What?"

"I think you're trying to scoop somebody else's man," Bethany says.

"Skip to the next track, Bethany. This song is played out."

"Look at you, using musical metaphors and stuff. Okay, just don't say I didn't tell you."

I roll my eyes. "I won't, Bethany."

"And don't think I'm gonna jump in if you and Dreya get to buggin', 'cause I don't get in family fights."

"Are you done?" I ask.

"Yes."

"Good."

My phone buzzes in my jacket pocket.

U miss me?

I laugh out loud. Sam is a trip.

"Who is that?" Bethany asks.

"You don't wanna know," I reply.

I send a response to the text.

Hahahaha. Y? u miss me?

"It must be Sam, then, if you won't tell me," Bethany fusses. "But I just told you I don't care about him. He's ugly anyway. Looks like a camel or something with that big old nose."

I roll my eyes in Bethany's direction. "I thought you said you were done."

My phone buzzes again.

I do, but Big D misses u more. Meeting tonight. I'll scoop u from school. What time u get out?

3:15. C u then, I respond.

A meeting? I wonder why Big D is involving me in a meeting. Does that mean I'm on the team? And if so, does that mean team Drama? Ew. I don't know if I want to be on that team.

It also didn't get past me that Sam said he misses me. Awwww. I might have to upgrade him to boyfriend status.

"Here come Truth and Dreya," Bethany whispers.

"Act like you don't see them," I whisper back.

"Too late."

Dreya says, "Sunday, you're riding with us to the studio after school, so be outside right at the end of last period."

She sounds irritated that I'm supposed to be riding with them, but Truth beams a gigantic smile in my direction. Dreya can't see him cheesing because he's standing behind her, with his hands around her waist and looking over her shoulder. His locs are hanging free, with a few stray curls teasing his hairline.

"Um, that's okay," I reply. "Sam is coming to pick me up."

"Well, that doesn't make any sense, when I'm right here. Text him and tell him you'll ride with me," Truth says.

"He wants to pick me up."

"Text him," Truth insists.

"Baby, if she wants to ride with him, that's cool," Dreya says. Even though she's trying to be sweet by saying *baby*. I can hear the irritation in her tone.

"Sam your boyfriend now?" Truth asks.

Dreya snatches herself out of his arms and asks, "Why do you care?"

"I don't," he chuckles. "I'm just being nosy. Guys gossip, too, you know."

"That's real thuggish of you," Bethany comments.

Dreya steps to Bethany and gets so close to her face that Bethany can probably smell what she ate for lunch. "What you tryin' to say, Bethany?"

"Nada," Bethany says quickly.

She's such a punk. There's no way Dreya would step to me like that out in public without me bringing it.

"You got one more time to say something about *my man*," Dreya says. "You gon' mess around and get hurt."

"You're tripping," Bethany says as she grabs her tray and walks away, leaving me standing in line.

"You betta get your girl," Dreya says to me.

"Last time I checked, she was your girl, too," I reply. "Don't start acting new, Dreya."

"My girls don't push up on my boyfriend," Dreya replies.

"I didn't see her pushing up on Truth," I say.

I stop short of saying that Truth offered to fix Bethany's plate that day, and that he openly flirts with me. But Dreya's not in a place where she would even believe me if I did tell her.

Not surprisingly, Truth looks like he's enjoying this little beef. Dudes like him always start stuff between girls and never take the blame. Dreya will be somewhere mad at her friend from way back and grinning up in his face.

"I'm riding with Sam," I say, following Bethany to the table. "See y'all at the studio."

11

"Epsilon Records wants to sign Drama to a three-record deal," Big D announces.

The room is silent for a moment. Sam, Truth, Dreya, and I are all in Big D's lounge with Shelly doing her usual chill move off in the corner. Big D grins at all of us, like he's waiting for someone to say something.

Truth jumps up and hugs Dreya. "That's what's up!"

"I thought they were gonna wait for Truth's single to drop first," Sam says.

"They were, but after we leaked the track, there were over a hundred thousand downloads on iTunes," Big D explains.

"I didn't know it was on iTunes!" Truth says.

Big D holds the sides of his extra large stomach and laughs. "Come on, now. You didn't think I was gonna leak a track and not make it available for purchase, did you?"

"You're a genius, man," Truth says. "Sorry I doubted you."

Truth then shocks the dummy out of me by kissing Big D on the cheek. What in the . . . ?

"It's a sign of respect," Sam says to me. "I see you looking twisted."

"I'm not looking like anything! I don't care who Truth kisses. Dreya might, but I don't."

This causes everyone to burst into laughter.

"Sunday, you're a real chick, you know that?" Truth asks.

Big D strokes his dark beard and continues. "I called y'all here because Epsilon wants to send Drama on the promotional tour with Truth. She'll open up the show for him."

"I don't even have a single out, though," Dreya says. "I thought I was just going on tour as Truth's girl."

Big D laughs out loud. "The record company doesn't pay travel for wifeys, baby girl. Especially for artists who haven't even blown up yet."

"What cities are we going to?" Truth asks.

"Atlanta, Chicago, Detroit, Charlotte, Birmingham, Orlando, Boston, and then to New York to be a part of a new artist showcase on *106 & Park*."

"We're gonna be on BET?" Dreya squeals.

"Yeah. You're gonna perform Truth's single, though. Nothing from your album. He was already booked, so this is Epsilon getting more bang for their buck."

This is all good news for Dreya, but I'm wondering why I'm here. "Congrats, y'all," I say, "but what's this got to do with me?"

Big D rubs his hands together. "Well, I went by your house to get Drama's mother to sign the contract and it was all bad."

Sidebar. It's totally iggin' me that Big D refuses to call Dreya by her real name. She's not on stage right now! And all of this is happening too quickly. We only met Big D a few days ago and now he's got Dreya a record deal. Internal alarms are going off in my head, but I tell them to be quiet because we're about to blow up!

"What do you mean, all bad?" Dreya asks. "She didn't sign?"

"She doesn't trust me; thinks I'm a drug dealer," Big D says.

"Still trying to figure out how I fit into this picture," I say.

"I suspect that you're the responsible one between you and Drama, so I need you to convince your aunt to sign the contract," Big D says.

"Once Aunt Charlie makes up her mind about something, it's pretty much a wrap."

Dreya says, "She's just paranoid because of what happened to Carlos! I can't believe she's gonna try to block my deal. I'll forge her signature if I have to."

"No, sweetheart. Epsilon does not roll like that," Big D replies. "They'll ice your career completely if you try to pull some stuff like that and your mama tries to press charges or sue."

"I don't know if this has anything to do with Carlos," I say. "I think it has more to do with you moving over here without asking permission."

Big D frowns. "You said your mother was cool with that."

"She is cool. Shut up, Sunday." Dreya shoots me a look that could kill.

"And what's the deal with Carlos? Who is he? What's that about?" Big D asks.

My lips are sealed. It's not my place to tell Big D my mother's business. Plus, I don't think he needs to know that.

Too bad me and Dreya are not on the same page.

She blurts, "Carlos is Sunday's mother's boyfriend. He just got shot by them thugs that own Club Pyramids in Decatur."

"I host parties there," Big D says. "Do y'all know what the beef was? Maybe I can help."

Everyone looks at me. I sigh and spill an abbreviated version of the story. "He was trying to buy into the club. His baby mother's brother is one of the owners. Something popped off—I don't know why—but he ended up shot. Now he's missing."

I don't tell Big D about Carlos losing my college tuition. It seems like that might be too much information for him right now. I can't have him knowing how desperately I need money. Desperation is not a good look at all.

"Oh, yeah. I heard something about that," Big D replies. "That's kinda sticky right there, so I don't wanna touch it."

"Good, because my mother would trip that I'm even telling you this," I say.

"How about if you go on tour with us?" Big D says. "Do you think that will change her mind?"

"I've got school," I respond. "I can't. I'm about to send in my application to Spelman. I can't take off."

"You'd only miss a couple of days. It starts the weekend before Thanksgiving, and goes through the following weekend."

"We're playing big venues in the middle of the week?" Truth asks.

Big D laughs. "Y'all are doing malls and teen clubs. You aren't big-venue status yet. We wouldn't sell any tickets."

"You said we sold a hundred thousand downloads of my single. That's not big-time?" Truth asks.

"Soon, but not yet. That's one single. People won't buy a concert ticket for one single."

I ask, "What am I going to tell my mother and aunt that I'll be doing on the tour? I don't have a record deal."

"Epsilon Records will pay for Drama to have an assistant on the road. You'll get a check, and you get to kick it to all the parties."

"I'll be Dreya's *assistant?*" I don't like the sound of this at all.

"Yeah, you'll get Drama's food and beverages, help her in the dressing room and all that."

I'm tripping. "She's not a star. Why does she need an assistant, Big D?"

"Apparently Epsilon Records thinks so. They heard the vocals on that CD and are trying to make her the next Keyshia Cole."

Sam clears his throat. "They heard Sunday's vocals mostly."

"Mostly nothing!" Dreya fusses. "She did a few ad-libs and runs. That's nothing."

Big D lifts an eyebrow. "Drama's the one with the look and the swagger to put us on the map. She's the one who's gonna blow up Truth's single. Y'all know the kids be on the hooks. They don't care 'bout no lyrics, or vocals even. Then, once all the girls see Truth on stage in his wifebeater and saggin' jeans, it's on and poppin'. Instant celebrity status."

Big D sure likes to paint a mental picture. It's just that I don't see myself anywhere in that little celebrity fantasy.

"So you think if I tell my auntie and my mother that I'm going on tour with y'all that they'll be cool with it?" I ask.

"I think so."

"How much is this check gonna be? Being this chick's assistant isn't gonna be easy."

Big D laughs again. "How's seven hundred for the whole tour sound?"

"Seven hundred? Man, please. That's a drop in my bucket."

"Well, you can't make more than the headliners, and they're only getting two thousand apiece for six shows."

"I don't know if that's worth the trouble."

Big D says, "Think about it. The summer after Drama's album drops, Epsilon is planning to do a real tour. They're already working on getting sponsors lined up. I'm talking twenty cities, and you get to roll."

"How much will I make then?"

"Thousands. But it all hinges on Drama's mother signing this record deal."

"Is Sam going on tour, too?" I ask, not wanting to do this thing alone.

"Awww . . . she wants her boo to come on the road, too," Truth teases.

Sam blushes and Big D has a really good gut laugh. "It's cool, Sunday. Sam is one of my engineers. Your man will be there."

I decide it's in my best interest not to argue here. I'm sure anything I say will only make us even more embarrassed. But I wish Sam would wipe that stupid grin off his face. He's not my man. Not yet anyway.

"I don't want her making thousands off my tour," Dreya says. "I turn eighteen in April. Why can't Epsilon Records wait until then?"

"You gotta strike while the iron is hot in this business. By the time April rolls by, they'll be on to the next new starlet. This might be your one shot."

So everybody's looking at me again, like all of this hangs on my head. The tour is after my college application deadline, so it won't interfere with that. And I guess if I ask my teachers I can get my classwork turned in early. Sometimes being a teacher's pet can come in handy.

"Okay, I'll ask my mother and my auntie. But I'm not making any promises."

Dreya says, "I'm going with you. I'm not leaving my career up to your hating self."

"You've already messed it up enough, Ms. Drama. Fall back and let your cousin do her thing," Big D advises.

"Yeah, and anyway, why would I do that? You make money, I make money. Don't forget that me and my man here wrote all the songs on your little release. I'm trying to blow up just like you."

"Thank you for claiming me," Sam says.

Everyone bursts into laughter, including me this time. But while everyone is so jolly, I'm not so sure I'm persuasive enough to convince my mother and Aunt Charlie of anything.

Maybe we should pray now, laugh later.

12

I've been waiting all evening, ever since Sam dropped me off from the studio, to bring up the subject of Dreya's contract to Aunt Charlie and ask my mother about going on tour, but they are in an uproar. My mother's been crying nonstop ever since she found out that Carlos is missing. And Aunt Charlie's been cussing and fussing about Big D.

"Have you heard from Dreya?" Aunt Charlie asks me. "She doesn't call me, like she's grown or something. I'm gonna call the police to go over there and charge Big D with kidnapping. He's probably got her hooked on drugs or something like that."

Here's my opening. "Big D is not like that, Auntie. He's legit, for real. He's got a state-of-the-art studio and everything. He's got a bunch of artists on his label."

"Yeah, he told me about Big D in the A Records, or whatever he calls it. I'm not feelin' it."

"He got Dreya a record deal, Auntie. With Epsilon Records."

"So what? I ain't never heard of no Epsilon Records! What's that supposed to mean to me?"

"Have you heard of Mystique?"

Aunt Charlie smiles, stands to her feet, and starts doing a little booty shake. "Yeah, baby. That's the girl that sings, 'My name is wifey, my name is wifey, my name is w-w-w-wifey.'"

She would pick Mystique's most terrible song. The video is even worse. She's dressed in a tuxedo and a bridal gown and marrying herself. It's insane, I tell you, but Mystique is a platinum-selling artist, so what do I know.

"Yes, Aunt Charlie. That's the one. She's signed to Epsilon Records."

"For real? Dreya's gonna be on BET?"

"Yes, but her stage name is Drama."

Aunt Charlie slaps her leg and laughs. "We 'bout to get paid? Is that what you telling me, Sunday?"

"We will if you sign the contract. They're not going to wait around for Dreya to turn eighteen."

Aunt Charlie holds her hand out. "Give me this contract. Let me read it."

I hand her the stack of papers from the table. "It's really pretty standard. They want to sign her to a three-record deal. She'll make two percent off the record sales, but make the most money off her tour."

"And how do you know it's pretty standard, smarty-pants?"

"Because my mom bought me *Everything You Need to Know About the Music Business*. It's all good, Auntie."

I watch as Aunt Charlie's eyes skim the document. She doesn't really know anything about the legal wording used on the contract, but she's reading every page anyway.

"The contract sounds like a good idea, but I don't think I like her living over there, though," Aunt Charlie says. "Tell her I'll sign it if she moves back home."

I bite my lip slowly, trying to think of a rebuttal. Dreya has no intention of moving back here, and I don't know how to convince her.

"At least until she turns eighteen," Aunt Charlie adds. "Then she can do whatever she wants. I just want to make sure my child is safe."

I nod and dial Big D on my cell phone. I think Aunt Charlie's request is reasonable and I know that he'll agree.

"Big D here."

"Hey, Big D, this is Sunday."

"My miniature hustla. What's up, baby girl?"

"Dreya's contract."

Big D clears his throat. "Break it down for me."

"Well, my aunt says she'll sign it on one condition."

"She wants more money?" Big D asks. "Because that's not doable. Epsilon Records is firm in that offer."

"Slow down! It's not money," I reply.

"Then what is it?"

"She wants Dreya to move back home. She doesn't like her living over there with you."

Aunt Charlie crosses her arms and nods in agreement. My mother even takes a break from sobbing to listen to the conversation. She gets up from the table and stands behind Aunt Charlie.

"Oh, is that all?" Big D asks. "Drama is on her way back to the house."

"You haven't even said anything to her yet!" I say. "What if she won't come back home?"

Big D replies, "Like I said, Sunday, she's on her way home. Please give your aunt my apologies for the whole situation. I would've never let her come if I'd known she didn't have permission."

"Why don't you come over and tell them yourself? I think my mother wants to meet and talk to you, too."

Big D takes a long pause before replying. "Are your mother and aunt listening to you on the phone now?" he asks.

"Yes, they are."

He sends an audible sigh over the phone. "Okay, Drama and I are on our way."

"Good! See you when you get here."

I press End on the phone and Aunt Charlie asks, "So?"

"He's bringing Dreya home."

Dreya storms into the house like a hurricane hitting the Gulf Coast. She doesn't speak to anyone; just goes straight to our bedroom. And Big D is looking too stressed, as if Dreya lived up to her stage name on the way over. Drama is what Drama does.

Big D extends his hand for Aunt Charlie to shake.

"Good evening, ma'am. I'm Deionte Silver, also known as Big D around Atlanta."

Deionte? Wow. I didn't know that was Big D's name. That is such an ungangsta kind of name. It makes me look at him in a totally different light. Like for real, Deionte sounds like someone's grandchild's name. Can't you imagine a grandmama saying, *Deionte, baby, get over here and give your grandmama some sugar?*

Aunt Charlie does not shake his hand. She looks him up and down and asks, "How much drugs have you sold to get this little music thing off the ground?"

Did someone say that this was a good idea to have the two of them meet? Oh, that was me? Well, then I totally take that back. Bad idea.

"Actually, ma'am, I've never sold any drugs."

"Well, then where'd you get the money to do all these tours and photo shoots and other mess? And how old are you, anyway? You don't seem old enough to be *the man* all like that."

Big D calmly replies, "Ma'am, I'm twenty-eight years old. I started planning parties my freshman year of college. I invited celebrities to come to my parties, advertised them, and split the money with the club owners. It was actually a good way for a student to make money."

"Where did you go to school?" my mother asks.

"Georgia Tech, ma'am. Played football, but I blew out my knee junior year."

"Well, if it was so easy, why didn't the club owners just do it themselves? Why'd they need you?" Aunt Charlie is not easily convinced and neither is my mother. I hope Big D came with his A game tonight.

"The clubs I worked with were owned by rich, older men who don't know what kids like. I made their clubs hot with my charisma and contacts, so it was all love."

"So you purchased a recording studio with the money you made throwing parties?" my mother asks. "I'm in the wrong business."

Big D flashes her a smile. "It's actually harder than it sounds, but yes, pretty much."

"So what makes you and this record company think Dreya is ready for the spotlight?" Aunt Charlie asks.

"She's good, and kids have already started downloading a song with her vocals on it."

"What song?" my mother asks. "And why was there no contract done for that? How much money did she receive?"

Big D responds, "The song is called 'What Ya Gonna Do,' and she sings the chorus. She received five hundred dollars for her work."

"That's all? What about royalties?" Aunt Charlie asks.

"It's called a work-for-hire agreement, and she won't receive royalties on that particular song, but she will off her album. Sunday and another guy named Sam wrote the songs for the album. Your daughters are very talented."

My mother looks at me. "Sunday, you didn't tell me you were writing music for this man. Where's your contract? And I thought y'all were a singing group. How is it that Dreya is the only one with a record deal? What about Bethany? And where's the money you got?"

"My money is in the bank, Mom. I opened a student account. You can call it my college fund."

My mother looks at the floor guiltily, but I don't take it back. I know she's not about to knock my hustle when my college fund just went up in smoke.

"These girls are minors," Aunt Charlie says. "All this under-the-table dealing is not cool. Somebody needs to do a better job of breaking this down for me."

I look at Big D and politely give him the floor. He explains all of this much better than I do, and he's got a way of speaking that will convince anyone. By the time he's done, he'll have my aunt and my mother buying swampland in Florida if he's selling it.

While he's talking, I wander back to my bedroom to make sure Dreya isn't destroying anything of mine. She's madder than a dog chained up one inch away from the mail carrier. Plus she gave me a really heated glare on her way into the house.

Dreya is sprawled across her bed when I open the door. She still looks angry, but I can't see that anything in my room has been trashed. That's a good thing for her, because I'm so not in the mood for delivering a beat-down.

"What?" she asks.

"Who said I wanted anything? Maybe I'm just coming back to my room to chill."

"I thought you and Big D were partners. Why don't you go up there and help get my record deal signed?"

"Are you for real? Big D asked me to soften up Aunt Charlie. You ought to be happy I did it!"

"I guess."

I sit down on the edge of my bed and stare at Dreya. She truly looks upset. "Are you mad that you can't stay over there at Big D's house with Truth?"

"It's not fair."

I want to tell her she sounds like Manny when he can't eat cookies before dinner. She even looks like him, with her eyebrows furrowed and her bottom lip poked out. This is soooo not the look of a diva right now.

"Dreya, suck it up. You're about to go on tour and get a record deal. Just be grateful for all this stuff that's happening to you. Lord knows you didn't do anything to deserve it."

Dreya sits up in the bed and narrows her eyes. "What do you mean, I don't deserve it?"

I know she didn't just ask me that. Time for a reality check, Sunday smackdown–style.

"Let me see. You're mean, hateful, disrespectful, and oh, your attitude stinks like a sack of dirty diapers."

"You're just jealous! You think it should be you with the record deal."

I shrug. "I'll get my own shot. And you better believe I won't blow it by throwing tantrums like a two-year-old."

Dreya narrows her eyes and jumps up from the bed. She storms back up to the front of our house with me behind her. I don't know what she's planning to do, but it can't be anything good.

"I don't want Sunday going on tour with me!" she announces. "She's a hater and her negativity ruins my creativity."

Big D looks at Dreya and bursts into laughter. Dreya frowns. But when my mother and aunt join in on the laugh fest, Dreya fumes.

"Sunday is part of the package, Dreya," Aunt Charlie

says. "You're not going anywhere without her, since you've proven that I can't trust you."

"What if I refuse to have her?" Dreya asks.

"Then this contract is going right in my paper shredder," Aunt Charlie says. "Don't try to play me."

Dreya balls both of her hands into fists, goes out the front door, and slams it.

"It's okay. She'll be back," my mother says.

"I know it," Big D says. "I've got a signed contract that says she will."

I don't know about my aunt and my mom, but a chill just ran up my spine. Dreya not wanting me to go on tour with her could definitely make my life complicated. So is all this really a come-up for me or is there drama on the next track?

13

*"Change me, rearrange me / got that photograph
you gave me / Somebody come and save me / you
got me going crazy. / You got me going crazy."*
—Sunday Tolliver

When you were little did your mother ever tell you
that the police were going to lock you up and put
you in jail when you misbehaved? That always used to
work on me and get me to straighten up quickly. It also
gave me an irrational fear of police officers. Even if I'm
driving nineteen miles per hour in a twenty-miles-per-
hour zone, I still look in my rearview mirror when I pass
a police officer.

So imagine how badly I want to run away screaming
when two uniformed police officers show up at my school
wanting to talk to me. They didn't say anything loud
enough for my class to hear, but clearly the words *Sunday* and *shooting* were both said. That spooked my calc
teacher, Ms. Wheatley.

"Sunday, will you please step outside and talk to the
officers for a moment."

My first thought is, How do we know these are really

police officers? I mean, I've watched enough Court TV to know that people show up masquerading as officers all the time, just so they can snatch people. If you ask me, these two look pretty suspect.

I step into the hallway with the officers, but I keep looking back over my shoulder waiting for someone to rescue me. My supposed-to-be ex-boyfriend, Romell, is leaning all the way out of his chair to see what's up, but is he trying to have my back? I don't think so.

One of the officers closes the classroom door behind me, and there's not one person walking down the hallway.

"Hi, Sunday. You haven't done anything wrong. We just want to let you know that up front," the first officer says.

"But you had to come up to my classroom? People are gonna think I'm a criminal."

Officer number two says, "Unfortunately, the questions that we have can't wait until later. We're trying to apprehend the shooter in the Carlos Acevedo case."

Duh! This is about Carlos. With all of the record-deal stuff going down, I forgot we're still in the middle of that particular unsolved mystery.

"Well, I wasn't at home at the time of the shooting. I didn't show up until the ambulances came."

"So you didn't see anything? Any suspicious cars or anyone unfamiliar in the neighborhood in the days leading up to the shooting?"

"No, but the day that Carlos got shot, I remember that his baby's mother, LaKeisha, called my mother about child support money."

Officer number one starts scribbling on his pad. Officer number two asks, "Did you hear the conversation? Was it an argument?"

"I didn't hear the conversation between my mother and LaKeisha, but I remember my mom fussing at Carlos about it before she left for work."

"So you don't actually know if the conversation took place?" officer number two asks. "You only think it happened."

"Why would my mother start an argument with her boyfriend over a fake conversation? That doesn't make any sense."

Officer number two doesn't answer, but officer number one continues to scribble details in the notebook.

"Do your mother and Carlos have a good relationship?"

I lift my eyebrows. What in the world does that have to do with anything?

"They have a great relationship. He lives with us, and they're going to get married when he has enough income to take care of us."

"So your mother wouldn't marry him due to his financial status?" officer number two asks.

"I didn't say that! You are putting words in my mouth."

"You said your mother fussed with Carlos about the mother of his child. Did they argue frequently about that?"

"Um, no. I thought you said you had questions about the shooting."

I wish I'd never brought up that argument, but I was

hoping that they'd start looking LaKeisha's way for some answers, not try to point the finger at my mother.

"Are y'all even close to making an arrest?" I ask.

"Thank you for your time, Sunday. We'll contact your mother when we have more information." So I guess I don't get to ask any questions, huh?

They walk away from me like they didn't come up to my school interrupting my day. I mean seriously, they could've asked me those questions anytime. They could've come to our house.

When I walk back into my classroom everyone is staring at me. I know exactly what they're thinking because I'd be thinking it, too. Police only show up at the school when it has something to do with drugs. Do they think I'm a drug dealer? If I was trying to be a rapper, that would probably help my career!

Since I'm totally stressed by my visit from the boys in blue, I grab my backpack and leave, telling my teacher that I have to go to the principal's office. She doesn't object; probably thinks I'm under arrest or something. And I was planning to ask her to write a recommendation letter for my college application.

On my way down the hall to who knows where, my guidance counselor, Mr. Brubaker, flags me down. "Sunday, can I talk to you for a moment?"

"Sure." I don't really feel like doing this, but Mr. Brubaker is the other person I need a recommendation letter from.

We go into his office, where Mr. Brubaker walks around the side of his desk and points to the chair for me to sit down. I plop down on the soft, worn-out leather. I bet thousands of students have sat in this chair because it's got a nice little dent in the middle where the behind should go.

"What's going on with you, Sunday? Be real with it, too, because I saw the police officers earlier."

I can't help but crack a smile at Mr. Brubaker. If he didn't have all that gray in his hair and beard, he'd be a grown-man hottie with that smooth, chocolate colored skin. But he's the coolest adult in this school, and I think the only one who really cares what happens to us when we leave here.

"I'm cool, Mr. Brubaker, but my mother's boyfriend is missing."

"I hope he's okay. Did you get that Spelman application done yet?"

I nod. "Almost. I still have to finish the essays and get my recommendation letters."

"When were you going to ask me for the letter, Sunday?" Mr. Brubaker gives me a knowing grin.

"I was about to today in fact! But then the police came up here and stole my joy!"

Mr. Brubaker throws his head back and laughs. "They stole your joy, Sunday?"

"Yes, sir, they did. Can I ask for your help with something?" I ask, my tone suddenly serious.

"Of course. What do you need?"

I shift a little bit in my seat, because I don't want to really put my mother out there, but I'm gonna need some help with my college fund.

"Mr. Brubaker, I don't think I'm gonna be able to go to

Spelman. I might have to do a community college for a few semesters, because my money isn't right."

"Have you applied for any scholarship money?"

"No, not yet. I don't even know where to start looking."

"You should've come to me sooner."

I shrug. "Up until a few days ago, I thought my mother had it covered."

Mr. Brubaker sighed. "Don't worry. We'll get you into Spelman and get it paid for. Your grades are excellent. I wish you did more extracurricular activities, but . . ."

"I do music after school, Mr. Brubaker. I don't have time for volleyball or the glee club."

He laughs out loud in his deep baritone. "You should join the glee club, Sunday. I could use your voice in the soprano section."

"Maybe. I'll think about it. When do you meet?"

"Thursdays before school and Saturday mornings. It shouldn't take too much time away from your other stuff."

"You might see me Thursday morning."

"Great. And, Sunday, I don't want you to worry about school. We'll take care of it."

"Okay, Mr. Brubaker. I'm trusting you on this one."

After school, Bethany and I meet up to get on the bus. She still doesn't know about the tour, and I'm trying to think of how to tell her about it without her blowing up.

"Dreya moved back home," I say.

Bethany laughs. "What happened? Did your Aunt Charlie go over to Big D's studio, wrecking shop?"

"No. Big D made her come back home so that Aunt Charlie would sign the contract."

"So there's a contract now? Wow . . ."

"Yeah, she signed to Epsilon Records."

"What about you? Did they give you an in-house song-writer gig?"

An in-house songwriter is someone who works for the record company and gets a paycheck like a regular job. They don't get royalties, though, so I'm not trying to go that route. I want to freelance like I've been doing. That's the only way for me to come up. Plus, what record company is trying to hire a seventeen-year-old?

"No, Bethany. I don't even want one of those. But they did give me a job."

"For real? Doing what?"

"Well, I have to be Dreya's assistant on two tours, photo shoots, and other stuff like that."

Bethany's mouth drops open like a broken hinge. "You have to be Dreya's assistant?"

"Yeah, it's cool."

Bethany doubles over with laughter. "That is *not* cool, Sunday. You are the leader of our group! You're used to being in charge. There is no way you're gonna be able to survive five minutes as Dreya's assistant!"

"That's where you're wrong. I'm doing this so that I can go on the road for free, meet celebrities, go to parties, and make money at the same time. I can handle Dreya."

Romell walks up to where we're standing. "Hey, Sunday."

"Hey, Romell. What's good?"

"You, girl. When we going to the movies?"

I crack up laughing. "You must like getting dogged out by girls."

"Nah, only you. Who was that lame that picked you up from school yesterday?"

"Wow. Hater much?"

"Naw, never that. I just wanted to know who you was kickin' it with these days."

That's really funny. "Ro, you didn't care too much when we were together, but now that we're apart, you all of a sudden checkin' for me?"

"Guess I didn't know what I had."

"Boy, stop. You don't mean that. What's up? You need help with your calculus homework or something?"

Romell sighs and his entire body relaxes. "Girl, I'm so glad you said that! I do need some help with the homework assignment."

"You can come over, Romell, and we can do the assignment together. All you had to do was ask."

Bethany covers her mouth and giggles. "If he comes over to your house, y'all not gonna do no homework. Maybe I should come, too, and chaperone."

Romell's eyes light up. "Do we need a chaperone, Sunday?"

"Uh, no. We do not, but, Bethany, you can come through if you want."

"Okay."

Romell narrows his eyes at Bethany like he's angry at her for some reason. I know he can't be over there thinking she's blocking, because there's nothing to block. I'm not feeling him at all anymore.

Romell licks his lips and runs a hand over his cornrows. "Bethany, you are a chump, for real. You stay in the way, don't you?"

"I'm in the way, Romell?" Bethany's feelings are probably hurt now. "Never mind, Sunday. I'll just go to my house."

"No, Bethany! He's just trying to psych you out. You're coming over."

Romell takes one of my long cornrows between his fingers and drapes it across my neck. I wonder if he likes my hair like this. I used to love when he played in my hair. Shoot, I still love it when he plays in my hair—I ain't gonna lie.

"No alone time?" Romell asks. His face is so close to mine that I can feel his fruity-scented breath in my ear.

I take a step back so I can clear my head. "No. No alone time, Romell. Just homework. I'm talking to somebody."

"You talking to somebody?" Romell repeats my statement as a question. "That dude who picked you up from school?"

I nod. "Yeah. He goes to DeKalb School of the Arts."

"For real?" Romell laughs in my face. "The *arts* school? You sure he likes girls?"

I roll my eyes. "Keep talking trash, and you're gonna be figuring out that calc homework by yourself."

Romell slides his hand over my hip. "Well, I just want you to know. I like girls."

"I know you do. Multiple girls, in fact." I push his hand away.

I'm glad the bus pulls up, because I don't want to continue this conversation with Romell. It's only going to end in an argument, because I can't help but get mad about all the times he played me for other girls. Only cute boys get away with that kind of stuff, though. I bet Sam wouldn't cheat on a girl.

Thinking about Sam makes me want to text him. I sit down in the seat next to Bethany and pull out my phone.

Hey, babe. What u doin?

A few seconds go by and he replies.

Thinkin' 'bout you. Want some pizza?

Dang. Now I wish I hadn't invited Romell over for homework.

Can't. Gotta tutor this dude.

Want some company?

I think it would be funny to see Romell and Sam interact. Romell and his hating and Sam with his perpetual cool swagger.

Yeah, come thru. And bring pepperoni.☺

14

For some reason, no one is home when we walk in from school. Not even Auntie Charlie and Manny, who are always here. Dreya's probably somewhere with Truth, so I'm not surprised that she's not home, and my mother's at work.

In a nutshell, we've got the house to ourselves.

"Nobody's home? See, I knew we shoulda kicked Bethany to the curb. It coulda been just me and you, Sunday," Romell fusses, and pouts like a little kid.

"Boy, please. Even if Bethany wasn't here, nothing would be going down. I'm not on you like that anymore."

Romell chuckles. "You think you're not on me like that. But I felt you shiver when I was playing in your hair earlier."

"That doesn't mean anything. It tickles when you do that. That's all."

I hear my own voice and it doesn't sound too convincing. No wonder he still thinks he's got it like that.

Bethany giggles. "Do y'all need me to leave?"

"No," I say a little bit too loudly. "Sam is on his way over here, and he's bringing pizza."

Romell frowns. "You invited your man to our study date?"

"This is not a date." I sit down at the dining room table and take out my calculus book. "Let's do this homework."

Romell skulks over to the table and sits down in front of me. "I know how to do the homework, Sunday. I just wanted to spend some time with you."

I cock my head to one side and really look at Romell. OMG, I think he's sincere. He silently takes his book and a sheet of paper out of his backpack. He looks at his pencil tip and it's broken, so I hand him a sharpener.

"Thanks," he mumbles as he sharpens his pencil.

He spreads his arms out on the table and leans closely into the book as if the words are too small. I don't know what he's reading, but he's sure concentrating hard. I always liked to watch him do homework like that.

Dang, why is he looking so good to me right now?

"I'm glad you came over," I say.

Just as he looks up and smiles, the doorbell rings. Who could that be? Oops! Did I really just forget that Sam was coming through? Wow . . .

"I'll get it," Bethany says. "You two lovebirds can just keep gazing into each other's eyes."

"Whatever." I chuckle nervously as Romell grins from ear to ear.

When Sam comes through the door, a breeze blows in the smell of pepperoni pizza and his cologne. He's all smiles, too, like he's happy to see me.

"Hey, Sunday and Bethany." He holds his fist out to Romell for a pound. "I'm Sam. What's good?"

Romell pounds back, but it's a halfhearted pound. "Yeah. I'm Romell."

If Sam can tell that Romell is heated, he doesn't let on. He comes around to my side of the table and hugs me from behind, taking in the back of the chair, too.

"I missed you, girl!" he says. "It feels like I haven't seen you in days."

"You just saw me yesterday, Sam. Do you have any homework to do?"

Sam shakes his head. "I finished it up in study hall. One of the perks of DSA."

"That might be the only perk," Romell says. "Y'all ain't got no football or basketball team that's 'bout nothin'."

"You might be right. I'm not all that into sports."

Romell leans back and blows breath through his lips in a whistle. "Is you a chick or something? This who you feelin', Sunday?"

"Yeah, liking sports would make me a real, down type of dude, right?" Sam asks, with sarcasm dripping from his tone like a melting Popsicle.

"Well, it would make you a dude at least."

Sam laughs. "Sunday, what do you think? Sports or music? What's more swagger filled?"

"Swagger filled?" laughs Bethany. "Oh, my goodness. Y'all are tripping."

"I'm not an expert on swagger. I can just say what I like, and Romell, you know I've never been on jocks all like that. You're the only ball player I've ever dated."

"So what you sayin'?" Romell asks.

"Well . . . I do like artists. Musicians, singers . . ."

"Rap dudes," blurts Bethany.

I'm looking at her real crazy right now. "What rap dude are you talking about?"

"You know! Truth."

Sam's face tightens. "You feeling him, Sunday?"

"Uh, nooo!"

I could bop Bethany in her head right now. She knows I don't want Truth. She's just trying to make both Romell and Sam mad at me at the same time. Obviously her hateration knows no bounds.

Romell turns to look at Bethany, who's flipping her long ponytail and sitting on the couch with her miniskirt hiked way up over her thick thighs. "She's talking to Truth, Bethany? The dude with the single?"

She shrugs. "I don't know if they're talking. That's Dreya's boyfriend. I just think that he likes her and they definitely flirt with each other."

Okay, wait a minute! Isn't she supposed to be my friend? I can't believe this. She's *that* mad about Romell and Sam both liking me that she would play me out with a lie. That's foul.

"Bethany, you need to stop playing. And you can step if you're gonna be in here lying. You know I've never flirted with Truth."

Bethany stands to her feet and puts on her jacket. "All I know is Dreya is checking for the wrong person. She needs to keep her eye on you instead of me, because I don't want that little troll-looking dude."

"You about to go?" Romell asks Bethany.

"Yeah. You wanna walk me home?"

Romell looks me up and down with a disgusted glare. "Yeah. It's all good. Your mother at the house?"

Bethany smiles. "Nope."

"Did you forget about Jordan?" I ask, reminding Bethany of her prom date.

"No. He's just my date, not my man."

Romell grabs his jacket and packs up his bag. "I'm out. Come on, Bethany."

"Enjoy my sloppy seconds!" I shout as Bethany walks toward the door.

I run behind the two of them and slam the door. Bethany gets on my nerves about these boys! Why can't we go back to the old days when we used to play jacks and listen to Destiny's Child CDs, before we even knew what they meant by "Say My Name." Her hormones have made her insane.

Sam opens up the box of pizza, takes out a hot, cheesy slice, and bites it. I try to gauge his mood as he slowly chews and swallows. I can't call it.

"I thought they'd never leave," he says. "Your friends are annoying."

"I know, right. I didn't know they were gonna trip like that. Well . . . I expected Romell to act a little bit stupid since I used to go with him, but Bethany's hating is out of the blue for real."

"You used to go with that dude? He doesn't seem like your type."

"Really? Well, then, what's my type?"

Sam freestyles. "Poetry-writing bruthas, who's respectful to they muthas, not pretty suckas, who quick to kick it with anotha."

"I like them rhymes you spittin', got me reminiscin' on the time when we was hangin'. S-sayin' you my type then?" I spit back with a flurry of giggles.

"Yeah, I'm your type." Sam's voice catches in his throat like he wants to say more, but doesn't.

The air is so thick in here now that I reach for the pizza box, trying to change to the next track. I need something upbeat right now. Some conversation to get us laughing, because Sam is staring at me with nothing but seriousness in his eyes.

"So it's gonna be fun going on tour, right?" I ask as I grab a slice of pizza for myself.

Sam chuckles. "It can be really fun. How fun do you want to make it?"

"Shut up! As much as Dreya gets on my nerves, I'm looking forward to this. We're part of a real live entourage."

"That's what's up!" Sam says, now joining in with the fun.

"Who else is gonna be on that BET new artist showcase?" I ask.

"I'm not sure who all of the artists are going to be, but Mystique is hosting it, and having an after party at Club 2020 in Brooklyn. It's all on the itinerary."

"What itinerary?"

Sam pulls a folded-up piece of paper out of his bag.

"Big D had me deal with the charter bus company that's doing the tour bus, so that's why I have this."

I read down the sheet of paper. This is about to be off the chain! Parties in every city at nightclubs where we're not even old enough to get in. Concerts at malls and expo centers.

"How are we going to get into these clubs? None of us are twenty-one."

"We have work permits for all of y'all. And they'll make sure you have on a wristband that says you're with the crew and underage. It's all taken care of. Epsilon Records handles all that back-end stuff."

"I can't wait."

"Me neither, but we've got a lot of work to do before we leave. That's about a month away."

"What work do we have to do? The music is already done, right?"

Sam laughs. "But your job as Drama's assistant is about to get real interesting."

I hold up a hand. "Wait a minute. I was supposed to be Dreya's assistant on the tour, right? What do I have to do beforehand?"

"We've got to go with the artists and stylists to pick out outfits, set up concert riders, get on Facebook to start a fan page, and give tour status updates. Plus, we need to activate Twitter accounts as Drama and Truth so that they can have little couple spats on the Internet."

I give Sam a blank stare. "Are you for real? I don't think seven hundred dollars is enough for all that."

"Stop thinking about dollars and cents, Sunday. You have to pay your dues first, and this is part of it. We're part of the entourage, remember? That's what an entourage does."

"It sounds like a lot of work."

"It can be a lot of fun, too."

I narrow my eyes at Sam. "Have you done this before, Sam? What other entourages have you been a part of?"

"None. This is my first one."

"So how do you know we have to do all this stuff?"

"Because I sit back and watch stuff. I'm an observer. I know exactly what we need to do to blow Truth and Drama up to the point where we can eat, too."

"Humph. Dreya is not trying to share the wealth. I promise you that if she's sitting at the top of the mountain, she's gonna be there all by herself."

Sam shakes his head. "She can't do this without you. That just reminded me of another thing you need to do when it's time for Drama to go on her summer tour."

"What's that?"

"You need to learn all of the words to her songs on her CD, exactly the way it's being sung on there. If there's a run, a pause, a hitch, you need to know it, because you're her vocal backup."

"Her vocal backup?"

"Yeah, Drama's voice is not strong enough to withstand a tour. It's gonna give out maybe more than once. She should be cool with Truth on this promo tour, though. It's only one song and she's only got the hook to sing."

"Dang. You observed all that?"

Sam chuckles and switches sides on the table so that he's sitting next to me. "You know what else I observed?"

His nose is nearly touching mine, and his breath feels hot on my face. The butterflies in my stomach are saying he's a little bit too close.

"What?" I ask, my voice as breathy as Sam's.

"This long string of cheese that you have hanging off your chin." He wipes my face with a napkin, jumps up, and laughs.

This tour is going to be an adventure.

15

"No, no, and are you kidding me? No!"

If Dreya turns down one more outfit, I'm going to scream! She has tried on at least fifteen ensembles and still hasn't picked one for the very first show in Atlanta. The executives at Epsilon Records want her to have at least seven outfits, including something fly for the Mystique-hosted party at the 2020 club.

"You expect me to wear *this* at my debut?" Dreya says. "This looks like I got it at some bargain basement. Stop playing."

The boutique employees scramble trying to put together new ensembles by throwing out more accessories, switching items around, and adding different pairs of shoes. They really want the sale, I guess, since Epsilon Records is footing the bill.

"And you're not even helping," Dreya snaps at me. "I thought you were supposed to be my assistant."

I reply by rolling my eyes. The only reason Big D sent me on this shopping expedition was to keep Dreya from spending too much money. He'd tried to explain to her that none of this was free and that the more she spent up front, the less she'd see when she got that first royalty check in the mail. But from the way she's snapping up designer goods, I don't think she heard him at all.

"We've been here for hours, Dreya, and you haven't chosen one thing. You've got rehearsal in two hours."

"Big D is tripping with these rehearsals. It's Saturday! When do I get a day off?"

A day off from what? She doesn't go to school during the week, doesn't do homework, and doesn't have a part-time job other than this record deal. So, I would say that just about every day is a day off for her.

"What are you doing over there?" Dreya asks. "Daydreaming about your little boyfriend?"

"I don't have a boyfriend at the present time, so I have no idea who you're talking about."

Dreya holds a BCBG skirt up to her body in the mirror and frowns. "You're not fooling anyone, Sunday. Our mothers always try to act like I'm the wild one, sending you with me on tour to be my babysitter. But for real, you're just as sneaky as I am."

"I don't sneak and do anything."

"It's whatever, Sunday. I won't tell anyway, so I don't know why you feel the need to hide stuff from me."

One of the store staff brought out a pink Baby Phat dress. For the first time since we've been in this store, Dreya smiles.

"I like," she says. "But what shoes am I supposed to rock with this?"

"How about these boots?" the salesperson asks.

The silver thigh-high boots are right up Dreya's alley, as are the chain-link belt, necklace, and bracelets that they add to the outfit.

"This can be my first outfit. One down, six to go."

I look at the price tags on everything she's already selected. Over seven hundred dollars on one outfit. Big D suggested that she not spend more than two thousand dollars on these outfits, and she's almost halfway to the limit after one.

"Dreya, you might want to find some other outfits to rock with these five-hundred-dollar boots. You're spending too much money already."

Dreya gives me an annoyed-looking head shake. "Sunday, stop being such a lame about this. It's all coming out of my money anyway."

I pick up a pair of skinny-leg Deréon jeans and a corset that are both on sale. The silver boots go perfect with the jeans and match the ribbon that ties the corset in back. Only an extra seventy-five dollars and I've hooked up a whole other look.

"I guess," Dreya says, turning up her nose at the corset.

"Five more. Let's go," I say. "Sam will be back in a little bit to pick us up for your rehearsal."

Dreya throws a few more tops and jeans on the table, a pair of black leggings and a black corset, red thigh-high boots, and several pairs of hoop earrings. It feels like she's bought up the store when they tell us the approximate total. She's got over three thousand dollars in merchandise already, and she's still rifling through the racks.

Sam's SUV pulls up in front of the store. A tiny smile graces my lips as he steps out of his ride. He's looking nice in his jeans, leather jacket, and Timberland boots. He pulls his skull cap down low and walks toward the store.

"Sam's here," I say. "You should probably wrap it on up. Big D will be upset if you keep him waiting."

"All right," Dreya says over a sigh. "I guess this will have to do."

While Dreya pays for her purchases, I step to Sam. "Hey."

"Hey. Did she buy up the store?" he asks.

"Pretty much. And she still thinks that she doesn't have enough."

Sam points at the pile of bags on the counter. "Looks like she has more than enough."

Dreya snaps her fingers twice and points at the bags. "Who was that for?" I ask Sam.

"I don't know. Maybe she hired a butler or something, because I know she wasn't doing that for us."

Dreya sucks her teeth in our direction. "Can y'all come get these bags?"

"We'll help you carry your bags, Drama, but you're carrying some, too," Sam says.

"What? Y'all are supposed to be my assistants. I'm telling Big D."

"Tell him!" I say. "Epsilon Records is not paying enough money for me to be a slave."

Sam bursts into laughter. "Okay, I'm gonna get the bags, but not because I'm your slave, Mz. Drama. It's because I'm a gentleman, and I won't have my girl carrying your bags."

His girl? When did that happen?

I watch silently as Sam loads up the SUV with Dreya's many bags. She slides a pair of sunglasses on and fluffs the front of her spiky, roosterlike hair. I'm not even going to comment on the fact that there is no sun shining at all. It's overcast and almost dark outside.

When Sam finishes with the last bag, he jogs up to the store and holds the door for me and Dreya to walk through. She sashays through and heads to the front seat of Sam's truck. The ungrateful diva doesn't even say thank you.

"Thanks, Sam."

He grins. "Don't worry about Drama. She's just feeling herself. I think it's funny."

I shrug and climb into the backseat of the SUV. Maybe Dreya would stop acting ridiculous if they'd call her by her real name. I don't think she's getting the point of having a stage persona.

"La, la, la, la, la, la, la, la, la . . ." Dreya sings up an entire scale and comes back down.

"Take it up an octave," I suggest, "and then I'll harmonize with you."

Dreya whips her head around. "This is not Daddy's Little Girls, Sunday. I don't need you rehearsing me."

I shake my head. "I'm just trying to help you."

"I didn't ask for your help."

"What's your problem?" I ask, getting tired of her attitude.

"You seem to have it twisted. You're not here to be my babysitter. You're supposed to be my assistant."

"And I'm trying to *assist* you. Maybe you didn't know that *help* and *assist* are synonyms."

She gives me a confused glare and turns back around to face the front.

Dreya doesn't sing another note all the way to the studio, which is completely stupid because she needs to warm up her voice. She has one of those voices that doesn't sound good unless it's warmed up. But since she won't listen to me, I'll let Big D tell her she sounds a mess.

To my surprise, and I think Dreya's, too, we walk into the studio and there are four girls in various shades of spandex doing dance moves with Truth. Well, Truth isn't really dancing, he's just standing there lip-synching the lyrics to his song.

"It's about time y'all got here," Big D says as he uses his remote control to turn off his iPod speakers.

"Sorry we kept you waiting, Big D," Sam says. "Drama had a lot of purchases that I had to load up."

Big D kisses Dreya on the cheek. "It's all good. Come on, Drama, you need to learn these moves."

Dreya laughs. "I don't dance."

All the chuckling and side conversations immediately cease. I don't know how many people have told Big D what they don't do, but based on everyone's reactions I don't think it's been many.

"What do you mean, you don't dance?"

"I mean I've got two left feet," Dreya says while looking down at her perfectly done manicure. "Ask my cousin. She knows."

Dreya is exaggerating a bit when she says she has two left feet. She can dance, but she has a problem with choreography. When we were in the group, Bethany would make up dance steps and Dreya could never remember them. So when we got on stage, she would just do whatever she wanted to do, which pretty much consisted of gyrating her hips and popping her booty.

Big D says, "You need to get over here and try this. I told Epsilon Records you were the total package, so don't mess this up."

"You said they thought I was the next Keyshia Cole. She doesn't dance," Dreya fusses.

"Think about who else they have on their label," Sam says. "You've got to keep up with Mystique, and she does it all."

Dreya stubbornly taps her chin with her long black fingernail. "Truth, baby, what do you think?" she asks.

"I don't dance either," he chuckles. "But I'm trying out a few moves. Maybe you don't have to do everything the dancers are doing."

I swallow a giggle. It's without question that she's not doing what these dancers can do. They're doing splits and leg stretches while we're deciding, and clearly they have some kind of training.

Big D presses a button and the music comes back on. The dancers start again, and Big D gives Dreya the signal to come over and start dancing. Sam and I sit down on the love seat to watch the show. I'm 100 percent sure it's going to be entertaining.

Dreya stumbles around for a few minutes, trying to get into the rhythm of the dance steps. It's pretty simple and repetitive choreography, but there's a lot of jumps and kicks.

"Do you think she'll get it?" I whisper to Sam.

"I don't think Big D really wants her to get the choreography. She's going to be singing the hook."

Now I'm confused. "So why does he have her doing this?"

"To humble her, I think. She's getting a big head way too soon."

I cover my mouth with one hand and smother my giggle. Big D's reason for making Dreya dance is making her pathetic moves even funnier.

Big D presses pause on his remote control again. "All right, Drama," he says. "I want you to belt out that hook while you're dancing."

"What?" Dreya shrieks. "Why do I have to sing? Truth is lip-synching."

"That's because I need him to save his voice. He's got a show tonight."

"He does? I'm not going?" Dreya asks.

"This is an underground thing," Truth explains. "Not doing radio-friendly tracks. What I'm performing tonight is pretty grimy."

"Well, I still want to go," she pouts.

Big D shakes his head. "Nah. I want your mother to be on board with everything we're doing with the tour. I need you to act like Sunday for the next few weeks. Go home early, no drinking, no wifey. And you could try doing some homework."

"Homework?" Dreya asks. "I haven't been to school in weeks."

"Well, you need to get yourself reenrolled. Epsilon Records is not thinking about signing a high school dropout."

"But my image is edgy," Dreya counters.

"You can be edgy with your hair and clothes. Having no high school diploma makes you a bad influence, and then guess what happens?"

"What?"

"Parents don't buy your record for their kids. School for you, ma."

Big D's broken it down so it could forever be broke! Dreya looks so twisted right now that it almost makes me feel sorry for her. She's got this image of what a celebrity should be, and Big D keeps bursting her bubble.

Sam hooks his arm through mine and pulls me up from the love seat. "Big D, me and Sunday are going down to the lab. I've got a track I want her to hear. You need us for anything?"

Big D grins at Sam. "Nah, dog. Get your game on."

Sam's blush reveals that he wants to do more in the lab than listen to some hot tracks. He's not slick at all.

The tiny room seems even smaller with Big D's remarks making the both of us tense. I take a seat on the piano bench while Sam turns on the keyboard and boots up his Mac.

"So when did I become your girl?" I ask.

Sam looks perplexed, kind of like a kid who bites into an onion thinking it's an apple. "What are you talking about? When did I say that?"

"Back at that boutique with Dreya. You said you didn't want your girl to carry her bags."

"Oh!" Sam says. "I didn't mean my *girl* like that. I meant like my homegirl, you know?"

"Oh . . ."

"Unless you wanted me to mean it that way."

I roll my eyes, I guess because I'm irritated and embarrassed. I thought that was just a slip when he called me his girl, and that he was thinking out loud about how he really felt. I guess I read the signs all wrong.

"I wanted you to mean what you meant. It's cool. You're my boy. Let's hear this track."

Sam pauses as if he wants to say something more, but clicks a few folders open on his Mac until the music file opens. The music fills the tiny room and practically bombards my ears with the strong bass line and syncopated drums. The mid-tempo tune makes you want to bob your head and chill at the same time.

"That sounds like a Mystique track."

Sam beams. "I'm so glad you said that! I want us to write a song for Mystique that we can give her when we meet her in New York City."

"Do you think we could write something that she'd want? She's big-time, Sam."

"Sunday, you write better than a lot of these songwriters out here. They write bubblegum stuff and your songs are soulful and deep."

With all these compliments, I can't help but smile. "Well, if we do this for Mystique, I wanna take my time on it."

"That's what's up."

"It's gonna be hot, though, I can feel it."

"It is. I know we can do this."

"We can totally do this."

"Sunday . . ."

"Yeah?"

"So when I said you were my girl earlier, I did mean it. I didn't just mean my homegirl."

I smile. "I knew you meant it."

"You did?"

"Yes. But I don't know if I'm ready to be somebody's girl."

" 'Cause I'm not a pretty boy like your ex?"

"What? No! That has nothing to do with it!"

"Oh. So what, then? Why aren't you trying to be my girl?"

I run my hands over the keys on Sam's keyboard. "When am I having my first piano lesson?"

"You changing the subject?"

"Yes, I am."

Sam sits next to me on the bench and strikes a key. "That's middle C."

I strike the key. "Middle C."

"Here's a very easy scale."

Sam's fingers fly quickly over the keys as he plays the eight notes of the scale. I try to pretend that his face isn't looking twisted as he does it.

"Sam . . ."

He looks at me, but doesn't open his mouth to say a word.

I continue. "I've got too much going on right now for a boyfriend, I think. But I do like you."

He nods and runs through another scale. "Now you try."

Sam takes my hand and places it on the keys. I try to imitate what he just did, and I almost do it perfectly, except for the last couple of notes.

"Good, Sunday."

"You're changing the subject?" I ask.

"Yes, I am. Let's just do the piano thing, okay?"

"Okay."

16

It's been two weeks since Dreya started going to school again, and a little over two weeks away from the Truth and Drama promotional tour. I think class is getting on Dreya's nerves, although she won't say it out loud. She's sitting at our dining room table struggling through her algebra II math homework.

"You want me to help?" I ask.

"I'd rather you just do it for me, Sunday."

I laugh out loud. "You'll never learn that way. It's just a little math."

"A little math? You know I'm not good at this stuff."

"Well, Big D thinks you need to graduate."

"Big D is not the boss of me. I signed a record deal with Epsilon Records, not him."

"So what are you saying?"

"I'm saying he works for me. Once I blow up and get a

few number-one hits, I'm gonna let him know what's up."

I lift my eyebrows and shrug. "Well, until then you should just try to do your homework. It's not that bad."

The front door opens, and it's my mother. The somber expression on her face makes me think that something is seriously wrong. I know before she says anything that it has something to do with Carlos.

"Hey, girls. Y'all doing homework?" my mother asks as she tosses her bag over onto the couch.

"I am," I reply. "But I don't know what Dreya is doing."

"Homework, too, Auntie Shawn. Stop being a hater, Sunday."

"Did you get that college application turned in?" my mother asks.

It really irritates me when she asks anything concerning school. She doesn't have the right to ask me about Spelman.

When I don't reply, my mother claps her hands together and says, "Well, I know you'll get in. Maybe this music thing will take off. If Dreya has a hit record, maybe she can help you get a deal, too."

This just completely burns me up! My mama is now pinning my hopes and dreams on Dreya's suspect music career? Doesn't she need to be coming up with her own plan B? Especially since I'm sure Aunt Charlie has some dreams that she's trying to relive. I could see her trying to go to cosmetology school to be a licensed lace-front wig applicator.

It's a good thing I've got enough sense to get my own thing popping. Waiting for a come-up from Dreya is like holding out for Oklahoma to become the hip-hop capital of the world. It ain't gonna happen!

Dreya rolls her eyes. "People always trying to come up off of someone else's success. Why don't y'all let me get mine first, before y'all start planning the hookups?"

Dreya snatches her books up from the table and storms down the hallway. I hope she doesn't think I'm trying to come up off her success. She needs to remember how everybody helped her. I've never heard of someone getting a big head so fast. She signs a record deal and starts acting ridiculous.

I follow her to the bedroom. "Why you always gotta be negative, Dreya?"

"Because I don't want to be here. Y'all can't force me to be here in this cramped up little Cracker Jack box of a house. When I get my advance check, I'm getting my own apartment."

"Who is gonna give a seventeen-year-old an apartment, Dreya? And you never had a problem with our house until you got this record deal."

"Yeah, well, I'm sick of it now. And I'm sick of this homework."

I shrug. "You need to chill before you mess up your big break."

"Don't you mean I need to chill before I mess up *your* big break? Sounds like you and your mother are already spending my money."

I turn to leave before I really say something to hurt

Dreya's feelings. I could tell her about how they would've been homeless without my mom stepping in. Or I could remind her how my mother is the one who bought her and Manny's Christmas presents for the last two years. Or I could call to mind how she wouldn't have any new school clothes if it wasn't for my mother breaking her back on her mail route.

But I don't say any of this, because that would cause drama.

Suddenly, I feel like I need some air, so I pull on my sweater to go for a walk.

Once I get outside, I pull out my phone to call Sam. "What you doing?" I ask when he answers the phone.

"Nothing. Was about to head to the studio."

"Oh, then never mind."

"Why? What you trying to do?"

"Wanted to see if you wanted to hang."

"Sure. Wanna catch a flick or something?"

"Nah, not in the mood for a movie."

Sam chuckles. "Okay, then, what do you suggest?"

"How 'bout we go to the aquarium?"

"The *real* aquarium? Like where the fish live?"

I giggle. "Yeah. I like fish. You gotta problem with it?"

"No. I'm on my way to scoop you. The aquarium it is."

Since I know it's gonna take Sam at least half an hour to get here, I continue my walk to blow off some steam. Dreya's made me real hot, so the walk and the peaceful fish will help me calm down.

As I hit the corner of our street and get ready to cross, a fly whip comes speeding past me. It's got to be a 1980s Cutlass Supreme with shiny chrome wheels and a spoiler. It's candy apple red and has to have about ten coats of wax, as shiny as it is. Nice.

The car does a U-turn in the middle of the street and rolls up next to me. When the window rolls down I see it's Truth.

"Hey, Sunday. Wanna take a ride?"

I shake my head. "Nah. I'm waiting on Sam to come pick me up."

"I thought your cousin told me you like old cars." He's got this look on his face like I hurt his feelings.

"I do like old cars. I love them."

"Well, then you've got to take a spin in this, baby. It's off the chain. It used to be my uncle's car before he died, but I had it restored with some of my advance money."

"You got advance money and didn't buy a new car?" I ask. "Most of these rap dudes out here are riding Bentleys and SUVs."

"I ain't got it like that yet. Plus, I'd still drive old cars, 'cause they ride smoother. You sure you don't want to take a spin?"

"I guess. A short spin. Sam is on his way."

Truth grins and unlocks the passenger door. Manual locks. Sweet!

I jump into the front seat and close the door. It even smells like an old car in here. Broken-in, soft leather seats and an Armor All shined-up dashboard. I close my eyes and inhale.

"I'm jealous," Truth says.

"Of what?"

"You got in here and inhaled, like you were sniffing up your man or something. I ain't never seen you that pumped when I walk in the room."

I burst out laughing. "Truth, why would I be pumped when you walk in the room? You are not my man."

"Still, I'm hot, so you should be pumped whether I belong to you or not."

"You're hot? Wow. You just sounded like Ray J talking to his crowd of chicken groupies."

Truth laughs, too. "Hey, don't hate on Ray J. I love that show. Ole boy be havin' them chicks scrappin' to be his girl. And he don't even want none of 'em in real life."

"I'm sayin'!" I agree. "Don't they know VH1 be giving out three show deals and whatnot? How could the girl on the first season think she was gonna last? He's got like two seasons to go."

"Yeah. That's almost a fantasy right there, though."

"What's a fantasy? To have a bunch of hoodrats scuffling over you?"

Truth shrugs as he hits the gas. "Nah, just to live in a mansion and do whatever I want, when I want. I'm gonna live like that, for real."

"Well, you're on the right track. After this tour, and that appearance on *106 & Park*, it's gonna be solidified."

"Yeah. Truth and Drama 'bout to be on the map."

Truth speeds past my house and keeps going. "You coulda dropped me off," I say.

"You don't like my company?" he asks.

"You're cool."

"So what I gotta do to get next to you?"

I blink a few times, wishing I had never gotten in this car. I've been trying to stay cool with Truth, without paying any attention to his game. I'm not interested, but I think if I come across too hard, he might find a reason to get me booted off the tour.

"Stop playin'," I reply. "You know you're into Dreya. She's been your girl for a minute."

"She don't have to be my only girl."

I chuckle. "So you one of those greedy cats, huh? Well, I like to be number one, and I don't share."

"I didn't think you would. But I'd be willing to bounce your cousin to the curb for you."

"Boy, stop. That's not the truth. I thought that's why you picked Truth for your rap name, because you're always honest."

He turns another corner too fast. It makes one side of the car lift off the ground. "I am being honest," he says. "I wanted to talk to you the first time I saw y'all group."

"So how'd you end up with Dreya?" I ask.

"You seemed like you weren't trying to holla, plus Dreya was pushing up on me."

"Well, you're with her now, and she's got mad love for you. What I look like, playing my cousin like that?"

Truth smiles. "So you sayin' that if me and Dreya wasn't together, you'd be my girl?"

"I don't know, but we don't even have to think about any of that, because you and Dreya *are* together. So can you please drop me back off at my house so I can meet Sam?"

"That dude is corny," Truth says.

"Don't be a hater. He's not corny. If it wasn't for Sam and his tracks, you might not have a record deal."

"Yeah, that's for real, but the dude is still corny. But you must like corny guys, because you all over him."

"Please, I'm not all over him. He's all over me. Don't get it twisted."

Truth drives back down our street and stops in front of our house. Dreya is standing on the walkway with her arms folded. She has a real heated expression on her face as I step out of the car.

"Hey, baby," Truth says out of the window. "Hop in and let's take a spin in my new whip."

She looks me up and down as I walk toward the house. "What you doing riding shotgun in my man's ride?"

"Oh, girl, stop tripping. You're the one who told him I like old cars. He was just letting me check it out."

"That better be all it was," Dreya says as she walks away.

Oooh. I'm this close to telling her how her man is riding hard, but it's not even worth it. We're about to go on tour and Sam will be here in a minute to take me someplace I really want to go.

As I walk toward the house I hear Truth say, "Girl, your cousin ain't got nothing on you. Come on here and let's ride."

I'm glad he's not my man.

A couple minutes after Truth pulls off, I see Sam's SUV rolling down our street. My lips curl into a smile all by themselves, because it's been a week since I've seen him. He's been busy getting things ready for the tour, and we've only been able to communicate by texting and on Facebook.

I jog up to the car and let myself in before he has time to jump out and hold the door. He always does that, but he can save his steps today. I'm ready to roll out.

"Hey, Sunday," he says cheerfully. "What's up with this aquarium stuff?"

"I love it! Seeing all that underwater wildlife is off the chain."

"Well, I hope you enjoy yourself. I got us some passes online before I left the house. It said you get to see all of the attractions and a 3-D movie or something."

"Yay!" I squeal. "You got the premium pass. But that's like thirty-five bucks. Thank you!"

"Well, I hope you brought some money for snacks," he says. "I'm tapped out."

"Even though I'm saving every penny I make, today I can do the snacks."

He laughs. "Oh, I forgot you're saving for your education! We can eat off the dollar menu at McDonald's. I'm not trying to mess you up!"

"Well, can we go to McDonald's first? I'm kinda hungry."

"Me too," Sam concurs.

I start to tell Sam about Truth pushing up on me earlier, but I don't know how he'll react. It's not like Sam and I are an official couple or anything like that. We're not even talking. It's just a friend thing for now.

He pulls up to the McDonald's drive-through window. "What do you want?"

"A double cheeseburger and some fries."

"Nothing to drink?"

"Yeah, a small orange drink."

Sam orders food for the both of us, drives to the second window, and hands the cashier a ten-dollar bill. "That's sweet. Two meals for under ten bucks!"

"Right, but when you blow up you better take me out to eat for real."

"Okay, so what do you mean by for real?"

"You can take me to Justin's or Pappadeaux or Sunday brunch at Pascal's. Any of those will do."

He laughs out loud. "You greedy, Sunday."

"No, I'm not! Just hungry. Give me my cheeseburger."

We smash our dollar meals on the way over to the aquarium, which is like a fifteen-minute drive. Everybody says that everything is twenty minutes away in ATL, but it's pretty much true.

Once we're through the security checkpoint at the aquarium, I'm ready to roll! I'm so hyped that Sam got the expensive ticket because I get to see everything.

"Which exhibit you want to hit first?" he asks.

"My favorite! Cold Water Quest. I want to see the beluga whales."

He laughs. "I'm mad that you know the exhibits by heart."

"You should appreciate the fact that I'm well rounded."

"I do, or I wouldn't be here with you. Somebody might question my street cred if they saw me bringing you here."

"According to Truth, you don't have any street cred anyway, so you don't have to worry about that."

Sam stops in his tracks. "He said that?"

"Actually he said you were corny, but who cares? I want to see the whales."

"He said I was *corny?*"

Aw, man. Maybe I shouldn't have told him that. I thought he'd think it was funny like I did. I didn't know he'd be standing up here taking it all personal and stuff.

"In my opinion, Truth is the corny one," I say, trying to smooth it over. "He's got this facade that's not even true, trying to pretend like he's hard, when he's just a lame with locs and tats."

"I'm not really tripping on him calling me corny," Sam says. "I'm tripping that he said it to you. Is he trying to wreck my flow? Why would he tell you that?"

I grab Sam's hand and pull him in the direction of my favorite exhibit. "Didn't I just say it doesn't matter? Let's go see the whales."

Sam gives a little resistance, but then he lets me pull him toward the door to the Cold Water Quest. It's dark inside, but the water is illuminated so that we can see the habitats of the whales and the area for the African penguins.

I stand in front of the whale tank, mesmerized like I always am. They are so big, but graceful at the same time.

Their movements are almost poetic, and when they talk to one another it sounds like music.

"Sunday, do you want to go to prom with me?" Sam asks, snapping me out of my trance.

"Prom? At DSA?"

"Yes, you know the thing we do at the end of senior year? Everybody gets dressed up in tuxedos and fancy dresses, we get in limos, eat rubber-chicken dinners and take pictures. Prom."

I laugh. "Sure, I'll go with you, but from the way you describe it, it almost sounds like you don't want to go."

"I do. I was just trying not to seem too corny."

"Boy, stop. Although it is kind of corny to get a prom date this early. It's not even winter break yet."

He pokes his lips out and nods. "I hear you. But everyone is already asking everyone else. I didn't want to take the chance that you might end up going with someone else. Like that Romell dude that was over your house."

"I don't even talk to him like that anymore. Bethany either—she's foul."

Bethany and I haven't had a conversation since that day she left my house with Romell. It's crazy, because we stand at the bus stop mean mugging each other instead of having our morning gossip sessions. But I can't deal with her flip-flopping. And she's especially been crazy since Dreya got the record deal. It's like hating to the infinite power or something.

"Are you going to ask me to go to your prom? Or am I too corny to show up with at Decatur High?"

"Oh, my goodness. I wish I hadn't even said that to you. Are you gonna be on that all day? Can we go to the next track, please?"

"All right, but answer the question."

"Yes, please go to my prom with me. We can rock the same outfits to both and save money."

Sam throws his head back and laughs. "You ain't playing about that college fund, are you?"

"No, buddy. If you hadn't asked me, I probably would've skipped the whole prom thing altogether."

"What?" he asks incredulously. "Every girl wants to get her hair done in some big updo, get her nails done, and go to prom. What's up with you?"

I point out my swept-to-the-side ponytail, jeans, layered tanks, jean jacket, and Timberland boots.

"Does this look like a girly girl to you?"

"No, but you do look like a hot girl."

I laugh. "Okay, I'll accept that. But when I get all that stuff done for prom, the hair and nails and stuff, it'll only be so that I don't embarrass you."

"My girl can wear whatever she likes to prom and I won't be embarrassed."

"There you go again," I say with an eyebrow-scrunching frown.

"There I go again with what?"

"That *my girl* stuff. Dude, don't say it unless you mean it."

Sam smiles slowly and pulls me into a hug. "Guess what?"

"What?"

"I mean it."

He kisses me softly on my lips and makes me believe that he means what he says. And the whales sing like they're enjoying the show.

17

Twitter is fun, when you're pretending to be someone else. And I'm pretending to be Dreya, or I should say Drama.

I never really got the whole point of posting little blurbs about your day-to-day life, but Dreya already has three hundred followers. I suspect that a lot of them are from our school, which makes this even more fun.

Countdown to the promo tour. ATL can catch us at Club Pyramids the Wednesday b4 Thanksgiving.

Truth hooked a sista up with gear galore. Go ahead and hate me.

I try to think like Dreya when I tweet for her. She's self-centered, rude, and doesn't care what anyone thinks of her. So she's pretty much liable to say anything.

One of her followers, ChaCha437, tweets,

Luv u on "What Ya Gonna Do"!

Do I know you?

I tweet back, thinking that Dreya would probably say something worse than that.
Then I feel bad so I say,

J/K ChaCha, cop that download on iTunes.

After I respond to ChaCha, a gang of Drama's followers start leaving congratulations messages. I do like Dreya would do—ignore them. I've got to go to class anyway. Got an honors English exam. I have to keep those scores up so I can get into Spelman.

I was so busy tweeting from my phone that I didn't see Bethany and Romell booed up at her locker until I almost crash into them. When she sees me, she gives Romell a disgustingly sloppy kiss. As if that will make me jealous. I don't care if they swap spit with each other.

But obviously her prom date, Jordan, does. He comes from out of nowhere and punches Romell in the back of his head, making him and Bethany tumble to the ground. Then Jordan jumps on Romell and starts whaling on the back of his head and neck until the security guards pull him off.

"You a slut!" Jordan screams at Bethany. "I can't believe I asked you to go to prom."

Bethany scrambles up off the floor, but Romell is motionless, like he's knocked out or something. "I don't care what you call me, Jordan! You need to get up out my face!"

One of the security guards tries to get Romell to his feet, but he's completely unresponsive. Then his body starts to twitch and his eyes roll back.

"Oh, my God!" I scream. "Somebody call 911!"

Then I realize I have a phone in my hand, so I do it myself.

"This is 911. What's your emergency?" says the 911 operator.

"A boy, he just got punched in the head a bunch of times, and now he looks like he's having a seizure!"

"Where are you calling from? I can't pin a location on your cell phone."

"I'm at Decatur High! Please send someone quickly! I don't think he's breathing!"

"Sweetie, is there an adult there?"

"Yes."

"Hand them the phone."

I give my cell phone over to one of the security guards. The other one has let Jordan go and is performing CPR on Romell. Now all the security guards are running down the hall, pushing kids out of the way.

After what seems like forever I hear sirens in the distance. But Romell is breathing again on his own, even though he hasn't opened his eyes. I was so scared he wasn't gonna start breathing again.

Bethany is crying hysterically and screaming, "This is all your fault, Sunday!"

I'm tripping now, because how is this my fault? If she hadn't been slobbering Romell down, trying to make me jealous, maybe Jordan wouldn't have jumped on him. Or maybe if she hadn't been playing these boys out here, then this wouldn't have happened. I'm feeling some kind of way about her trying to blame me for Romell, who is now getting carried out on a stretcher.

At least his eyes are now open. The paramedic is asking him questions, and he seems to be responding. Looks like at the worst he got knocked out by Jordan. I know this is not the end of this episode. Romell's ball-player friends are gonna get Jordan at some point. I see them eyeballing him down already. He might as well make his life easier and go ahead and transfer.

Dreya appears from out of the crowd and walks straight toward Bethany. She shocks me by giving her a hug and whispering something in her ear. Whatever Dreya says has Bethany smiling from ear to ear and hugging her back.

The security guards start clearing everyone out of the halls, so people start moving toward their classrooms. I grab Dreya by the arm as she tries to sashay past me.

"What did you say to Bethany?" I ask.

"None of your business."

I ask again, "What did you say to Bethany?"

"If you must know, Sunday, I invited her on tour with us. She can be one of my assistants."

"Epsilon Records isn't going to spring for another hotel room. So where is she staying? With you?"

"No. She's staying in the assistant's room with you."

I laugh out loud. "You getting payback for me riding around the block in Truth's car?"

"No, but I don't trust either one of y'all, so you don't need to have a hotel room by yourself. I'd have to hurt both of y'all if I saw him creeping to your room late at night."

"You can't be serious to think I would want him, or that I would play you like that. We're family, Dreya."

"Yeah, well, family does foul stuff, too. Like I'm still trying to figure out how you found a way to get a paycheck off my come-up."

"How about that tiny, tiny part of writing all the songs on the album? Did you forget about that?"

"I didn't forget. But once this album is a number-one hit, I'm kicking you and that corny Sam to the curb for my sophomore release. You're not gonna be making royalties off my career. Get your own record deal."

Dreya pretends to wave down some girls who aren't even her friends. Now that I think about it, Dreya doesn't have any friends except me and Bethany. She's either dogged out everyone else, stolen their boyfriend, or done something else just as foul.

And now she's bringing Bethany on tour with us. That's a real trip right there. I watch Bethany standing at her locker, laughing with one of Romell's friends, as if her new man wasn't in the hospital with a head injury. What Jordan did to Romell could be classified as blunt force trauma to the head. I learned that from watching *Law & Order.*

But like I was saying, Bethany on this tour is going to be drama to the infinite power. If Dreya thinks she needs to watch her back with me, she better double that with Bethany, because she's the one who's really looking for a come-up.

18

―――――

"You ready to record this song?" Sam asks from outside the booth.

I nod and smile. "So ready. Let's do this."

Sam and I collaborated on this song for Mystique, and I know when she hears it she's gonna love it. And it looks like we're going to have to make our songwriting mark without Dreya/Drama, because she's determined not to have us writing for her on her next record.

She even told Big D her suspicions about me and Truth. He reassured her that I didn't have anything on her; same thing Truth told her. It's a good thing I've got high self-esteem, because if I didn't, all this talk about Dreya being hotter than me might hurt my feelings.

Anyway, our song for Mystique is called "This Time." It's a midtempo breakup song, which is the type of song that Mystique always turns into a hit. I think she'll love it when she hears it. I'm going to purposely sing in her favorite key, so that she sings along after the first verse.

As you can tell, Sam and I thought this thing all the way through.

I hear the intro on the track filtering in through the headset. I close my eyes and get ready to belt the words.

I sing the first verse in a quiet, smooth voice. "Your new girlfriend called me up last night / Telling me that I better be movin' on / Didn't call you, 'cause all we'd do is fight / So instead I wrote you a little song."

Now I take a deep breath to transition to the bridge. "This time is the last time / you're breaking my heart / you've torn it apart / This time is the last time / I'm crying over you / crying over y-ou!"

The drums kick in loudly for the chorus, and my voice grows loud, too, emotionally belting out the sad words.

"This time it really is over.

This time not taking you back.

This time not thinking it over.

This time I'm packin' my bags.

This time I don't believe you.

This time ain't changing my plans.

This time when I walk out

This time not coming back!"

I don't open my eyes until I sing the second verse, bridge, and chorus again. When I do, Sam is clapping with an awestruck look on his face. Big D has joined him, and he's clapping as well.

"That was hot, Sunday," Big D says through the microphone. "Is that for Dreya's sophomore album?"

Sam lifts an eyebrow. "Nah, this is for Sunday's songwriting demo. Dreya doesn't want us working on her stuff anymore."

Big D frowns and waves for me to come out of the sound booth. I pull open the heavy wooden door and join them in the technical area of the room.

"Drama said she doesn't want you working on her next album?" Big D asks me.

"Yeah, she's on some mess. She thinks I want Truth, which is completely and totally not the case."

Big D shakes his head. "Y'all know what, bump her then. If she's tripping on her own cousin, it's only a matter of time before she's tripping on me. That song sounds like something Mystique would sing. Y'all need to let her hear it. She'll love it. It might just get you enough money for your tuition, lil' mama."

I don't tell Big D what Dreya said about kicking him to the curb after she blows up. For some reason, I feel a sense of loyalty to my cousin, and I don't know what Big D would do to her. I've not seen any evidence that he's gangsta, outside of his looks, but the fact that he keeps company with the thugs at Club Pyramids gives me pause.

I clear my throat. "Are you gonna try to take credit for it, too?"

"Since y'all secretly using my equipment to do this little project, I could," Big D says while stroking his goatee. "But this genius is all y'all. God would get me for trying to get in on that."

Sam chuckles. "This ain't had nothing to do with me. Sunday made an ordinary track come to life with her melody, lyrics, and vocals. I don't even feel like I should take credit."

"Of course you should," I say. "I got the idea for the song after hearing your track. The melody wouldn't have come to my mind without hearing your track."

Big D interjects, "While you two are in here stroking each other's egos, I'm gonna go and check on this dance rehearsal upstairs. Drama wasn't lying when she said she had two left feet. I'm thinking maybe I signed up the wrong cousin."

"My music and image wouldn't fit with Truth. Dreya is much better suited for that edgy, hip-hop thing they got going. I couldn't pull that off if you paid me. You wait until Dreya gets on stage, though. She can dance—she just can't do the choreography."

"Here's a suggestion for the track for Mystique," Big D says. "Don't add too many runs or ad-libs on your second go-round. Leave it clean. The melody is hot enough the way it is, and knowing Mystique, she'd want to finesse it in her own way."

"Thanks for the tip," I say, although I hadn't planned to do any ad-libs.

"Well, I'm gonna leave y'all to your genius! Make it hot," Big D says with a smile as he backs out of the music lab.

The song has a pop sound to it, but my voice makes it soulful. It's perfect for the kind of crossover music that Mystique does, and I really hope she's feeling it. Even if she doesn't, Sam is sure we can sell this to someone, and make some serious cash.

I sip from a bottle of water while Sam does some things on his magic soundboard. He's really talented with flipping those little dials and making sure the perfect sound emerges.

Speaking of emerging, why is Bethany standing in here all of a sudden? "What do you want?" I ask.

"Drama told me to check on y'all and see what y'all are down here doing."

I laugh out loud. "What are you, her little spy now?"

"No. She just wants to know what her staff is doing. She needed water and you weren't there to hand it to her. Drama was a little bit upset that she was thirsty and had to find her own water."

Sam asks, "What were you doing? Why couldn't you get the water, assistant number two?"

"Because I had to watch Shelly as she was preparing the food. Drama doesn't trust Shelly cooking for her, so she asked me to monitor the food preparation."

I'm searching Bethany's face for any sign that she's joking, and I can't find it. "Bethany, you need to tell Dreya that she's tripping."

"I don't know if she is. She's right to watch her back. Truth is a player. He's tried to get with both of us behind her back. There's no telling what he might do."

"Why doesn't she break up with him then?" I ask. "Why would you stay with a guy you don't even trust with your own cousin?"

"You know why, Sunday. It's for her career. She needs Truth right now to help her blow up."

Sam says, "She's messed up for real if she doesn't even trust her cousin."

"Well, she doesn't. That's the only reason why Bethany

is coming on this tour," I say. "What did you tell your mom, anyway, Bethany? They're cool with you taking time off from school to go on a tour?"

"Yeah. She wants me to get a record deal. She thinks I can be Miley Cyrus or Taylor Swift, and I do, too."

I think on this for a minute. Bethany *can* sing. Probably better than Miley and Taylor. That's the only reason why she was in our group. It would be crazy if she ended up with a record deal, too, but I'm sure Dreya will do everything in her power to make sure that doesn't happen.

"Have you heard anything about Romell?" I ask, changing this stupid subject. "Is he still in the hospital?"

"No, he got out. He just had a concussion, that's all, but Jordan got charged with assault."

"How do you feel about that?" I ask.

She shrugs. "Just two hardheads duking it out. It has nothing to do with me. Jordan knows that I wasn't his girlfriend. It's not my fault all this junk I'm packing makes the brothas go wild."

She giggles and sashays out of the room, making sure to give Sam an ample view of her behind on the way out. Sam rolls his eyes and shakes his head.

"No thank you," he says to the back of Bethany's head.

I laugh out loud. "No, thank you?"

"Yeah. I want her to know that not all the brothas only care about booties."

"Nobody cares what Bethany thinks. She's a lame. She and Dreya."

Sam plays on the keyboard, doing the beginning of our song. Every time we vibe on a song, I feel myself liking Sam even more. But I've gotta stay focused right now. We're right on the verge of something with this song, and I can't let Sam or a crush get in the way of me getting mine. That wouldn't be a good look at all.

19

It's the night of Truth and Drama's very first show! It's right here in Atlanta at Club Pyramids. We're launching the tour here, and immediately following the show, we'll be headed straight to Birmingham, then to Orlando, on the tour bus.

Everyone's been involved in the rehearsals for the past few weeks, but I still feel like they're not completely ready. First of all, Dreya gave up on learning the dance choreography. She just plans to freestyle her dance moves, since she's on the microphone anyway. Every now and then she'll hit a move with the dancers that actually looks kind of smooth.

I inhale deeply as I walk into the living room. Our entire house smells like turkey and dressing. We're having a Thanksgiving lunch today, since we'll be in Birmingham on Thanksgiving night. My mother doesn't play when it comes to the holidays. But I'm glad she's cooking for us early, because I'm getting my grub on. Good thing I'm not performing, 'cause I'd be sluggish as what with all that dressing and macaroni and cheese sitting at the bottom of my gut.

"Mommy, everything smells good. I can't wait to dig in," I say.

My mother sighs. "I just wish Carlos was going to be here."

"At least they haven't found him yet. Maybe that means he's hiding out from those dudes at the club. Y'all will get back together when this all blows over."

Aunt Charlie interjects from the living room, "Carlos ain't fooling me. He doesn't want to snitch on those dudes that shot him and he sure as heck doesn't want to start replacing Sunday's college fund."

"So you definitely think he's hiding out somewhere?" I ask Aunt Charlie.

"I sure do. He's probably back in Puerto Rico by now."

"He had too many injuries for that, Charlie. They shot him five times, remember?"

"Stranger things have happened. Plus, I've been thinking, what if Carlos wasn't trying to buy into the club? That's the story he told you, but what if he owed them money for some reason?" Aunt Charlie asks.

"The only thing that keeps me going is that he could be alive somewhere. But he was injured when he disappeared from the hospital, and the only money he had was stolen. How could he hide out for long with no money?"

"Maybe his family is helping him," I offer.

"His family? They haven't helped him before, so why would they be helping him now?"

I shrug. "I don't know. Maybe him getting shot was a wake-up call to them."

"There's no way Carlos would go into hiding and not get word to me. He loves me too much to let me go through this pain if he's really okay. If he would do that . . . then I don't think I know him at all."

Aunt Charlie adds, "I think there are a lot of things that you don't know about Carlos."

"Well, I invited his mother and sister over here for our Thanksgiving lunch. I don't even know if they're coming, though. They didn't respond. But can you clean up for me, in case they do?"

Luckily I've already packed for the tour, so I do have a few hours of free time on my hands. I start with the bathroom. I clean every fixture and remove Aunt Charlie's ashtray that's filled with cigarette butts and ashes. Then I empty the overflowing trash container. I wipe down the shower curtain, fluff out the little floor carpet, and spray some air freshener.

Then I move to the living room, Aunt Charlie's favorite hangout spot. I put away all of her bedding and sweep all the crumbs off the leather couch. I hate that Aunt Charlie's body has left permanent indentations in the couch, but there's nothing I can do about that.

I do a full dusting, sweep and mop the ceramic tile floors, and make sure the glass coffee and end tables are shining. Aunt Charlie doesn't move an inch to help either. She just lifts her feet up when I go by. That's just trifling.

"You could help," I say to Aunt Charlie.

"Girl, that's why me and your mama had kids, so we wouldn't have to do housework."

"Wow, okay. So y'all had kids so they could be slaves?"

"Pretty much."

"Well, I don't see your daughter doing any house-work," my mother calls from the kitchen.

Aunt Charlie laughs. "Y'all know Drama is too much of a diva to do housework. She don't roll like that. I ain't mad at her, though. She can't go on the stage with dish-pan hands."

"Mommy, are y'all coming to the show?" I ask.

She shakes her head. "Baby, you know I can't go up in that club. LaKeisha will probably be there with her brothers, just waiting to pop something off."

"Do you think the girls are in any danger?" Aunt Charlie asks.

My mother shrugs. "I don't know, but I don't like them going to that club either."

"Big D will make sure nothing happens to us. LaKeisha's brothers don't have any beef with us."

Aunt Charlie replies, "Big D is a nice-size dude, but he can't stop a gun, and we know those fools up at Club Pyamids are packing heat."

My mother rolls her eyes at my aunt's insensitive words. "Charlie . . ."

"What?"

"Nothing! Let's just get ready for this Thanksgiving lunch."

Everyone's here for the Thanksgiving luncheon, except Dreya. She had to do a final rehearsal down at the studio. Big D told her she'd have time to eat after the show. Plus, he didn't want her eating a heavy meal that would make her groggy, sleepy, and sluggish.

I invited Sam to join us, since he's gonna be on the road, too. He even brought a dish. A sweet potato pie that he made himself.

"That pie looks good, Sam," my mother says.

"I hope so. I used my grandmother's recipe."

"He can cook, Mom!" I say. "He makes this lasagna and pound cake that is off the chain!"

My mother kisses him on the cheek. "Well, my daughter is greedy, so I'm sure she appreciates a boyfriend who can cook!"

"He's not my boyfriend, Mom. He's my friend."

My mother smiles. "Well, he *should* be your boyfriend! What's wrong with you?"

"That's what I keep telling her," Sam says.

"Sam knows that he's not my boyfriend, because I have to concentrate on my grind right now. Just like he needs to concentrate on his grind."

"Who are you?" my mother asks. "I never knew you were so focused on making money. But maybe that's my fault."

I lift my eyebrows at my mother. "Maybe, just a little bit."

Sam laughs and puts his arm around my waist. He whispers in my ear, "Your mother is funny."

Manny pokes Sam in the leg. "No, sir. No whispering in our house. That is rude."

"You're right, little man. I'm gonna go over here and sit on the couch until we get ready to eat. Is that okay with you?"

Manny frowns. "You can sit on the love seat and Sunday can sit on the couch. Ain't no hanky-panky going on at our Thanksgiving lunch!"

I spank him on his little behind. "Boy, what you know about hanky-panky?"

"I know enough. And where is my sister?"

"Manny, Dreya is practicing for her show tonight," Aunt Charlie says. "She couldn't take time out to eat with her family."

Aunt Charlie sounds a little bit upset that Dreya's not here, but she better get used to her daughter being ghost, because Dreya plans on moving out of here in a few months. As soon as she turns eighteen.

"Everyone can come to the table now," my mother announces. "The turkey is ready to be carved!"

Everyone sits down at the dining room table, which usually only seats six. But we've added the extension piece and some card table chairs so that everyone can fit, including Carlos's mother and sister, who'd shown up, but don't look very happy. Even Manny gets to sit at the big-people's table today.

My mother brings out the hot turkey and sets it in the middle of the table with all of the other goodies.

My mother says, "Since I'm the only one who goes to church here on a regular basis, I guess I'll say grace."

A few snickers come from around the table, as we bow our heads.

"Dear God, thank you for bringing us together on a holiday that's all about giving thanks. We are grateful that you have provided us with this bountiful feast, friends, family, and health. We pray for Carlos's safety, and that wherever he is, he comes home to us soon, because we all miss him. Especially me. Amen."

I glance at Carlos's mother after my mom is done praying and she's got a really strange look on her face. I can't really decipher what she's thinking, but it makes me reconsider what Aunt Charlie said. Maybe they have helped him hide out from the guys at the club. That's cruel if they know he's alive and aren't telling my mother. That would be too crazy.

My mom slices the turkey with her electric knife. While she's doing that, we start passing the other side dishes around the table. Carlos's sister and mother both have sour expressions on their faces and neither of them say a word. I guess they don't really want to be here, but maybe felt obligated because my mother asked them to come.

"I hear your daughter has a show at Club Pyramids," Carlos's sister says to Aunt Charlie. "How can you deal with that club after what happened to my brother?"

Aunt Charlie scoffs. "This is my daughter's big break, and I don't have any beef with those dudes."

"Well, I have beef!" my mother says. "They shot my man."

"Exactly," Carlos's sister says. "But still you let your daughters go there?"

"Let's just eat this beautiful dinner that Ms. Tolliver has prepared," Sam says. "We're not here to talk about the shooting."

Aunt Charlie says, "You got that right. We're here to be thankful. And I am thankful that my daughter has a three-record deal with Epsilon Records. That little ghetto mess that Carlos has going on is not going to block my baby's success. You can best believe that."

Now everyone at the table, besides Manny, is looking crazy. Why can't we just have a decent family dinner without this hood soap-opera mess? I scoop huge helpings of everything on my plate and try to enjoy my food, but this little argument has put a horrible taste in my mouth.

One thing I do know for sure, though, is that Aunt Charlie is not going to let Carlos or anybody else keep Dreya from blowing up. She's got big spending plans herself. I overheard her talking to one of her friends about the whip that her daughter was going to get her when she gets her first royalty check. She's talking about a powder blue Lexus truck, and a two-story house in Lithonia.

It seems like everybody's hopes and dreams are resting on Dreya acting like she's got some sense and being the artist that Epsilon has signed her to be. I hope that she doesn't let everybody down, including herself.

20

Club Pyramids is jumping, jumping tonight. The majority of our crew is only allowed in a special nonalcoholic VIP section and backstage. Epsilon Records had to get special permits to allow underage artists to perform, and were only able to pull it off at Club Pyramids and Club 2020 in New York City. The rest of the stops on the tour will be mall shows, sponsored by whatever record store is in that particular mall.

It won't be glamorous at all, so Dreya definitely didn't need to spend three thousand dollars on clothes. The highlight of the tour will definitely be the *106 & Park* appearance and the after party at Club 2020.

"Sunday, where's my other boot?" Dreya fusses.

"On the other side of your chair."

For once, I understand why Dreya is a bit annoyed. This dressing room isn't bigger than a closet, and it's even smaller with Dreya's several outfit selections and Bethany and myself crowded in, too.

Dreya locates the boot and pulls it on. "Help me spike my hair, Bethany. You know how to do it with the gel, right?"

Bethany jumps up. "Of course, Drama. Do you want me to do your makeup, too? I don't know if the makeup artist is going to make it."

Dreya sucks her teeth. "That's what happens when I let Big D hire the help. When was the ghetto makeup artist supposed to show up?"

"An hour ago," Bethany says. "But it's all good. I can have you looking fine."

"You better."

"Yes, Drama. I will."

I gag and almost throw up in my mouth at Bethany's antics. Yes, Drama. Of course, Drama. Ugh! Doesn't the girl have any pride? Plus, she's not even getting paid for any of this. Her mom only let her come because she's just as thirsty as Bethany is for fame. Epsilon Records refused to pay another salary, and said that if Dreya wanted to give Bethany some money she could. Yeah, as if that'll happen.

Big D pokes his head in the dressing room door. "Drama, sweetie, you've got five minutes. Need anything? Water?"

"A Sprite if you can get one. Thanks."

"I'll go and get it," I volunteer. It'll get me away from Bethany.

I weave through the crowd and to our VIP area, where

there's a waitress. I ask her, "One Sprite, please. It's for Drama, and she only has a few minutes till stage time."

"Coming right up. Do you want me to deliver that to the dressing room?"

"If you could, that would be great."

"Sure."

The waitresses in this place are all built similarly to Shelly: thick, with big behinds and long hair weaves. I wonder if they have to put their measurements down on the application. And their uniforms are off the chain, too. They're all wearing tiny French maid costumes and fishnet panty hose. Pretty stank looking if you ask me, but the guys are loving it and the waitresses are getting some pretty nice tips.

"Is Drama almost ready?" Sam asks. "The crowd is pretty pumped."

"Yeah, she's almost ready. Dreya is a natural performer. She'll get pumped right with the crowd."

I head back toward the dressing room and notice that the waitress is on her way, too, with the Sprite. I do her a favor and take it from her. She doesn't need to hear any fussing that Dreya might do, about it being too cold, too flat, or whatever. Dreya's gonna drink this soda and be happy with it.

"Here you go, Dreya," I say as I hand her the Sprite.

She closes her eyes and takes a long sip. "It's flat," she says.

"This is all they had."

"Well, next show I want you to make sure to have a twelve-pack of Sprite in my dressing room."

"Why do you need a twelve-pack? There's only one of you."

Dreya rolls her eyes. "Don't stress me, Sunday. Just do as I ask. You're the assistant."

"Okay, whatever. A twelve-pack. It's your money."

"And while we're on tour, I want you to call me Drama. Everyone else does. It makes us seem too familiar when you call me Dreya."

"That's your name."

"Anyway. Call me Drama."

Let me get out of this room before I get to blowin' up on this girl. There's not enough room in here for me and her ego.

Backstage, I pull up Twitter on my phone and post a status update from Ms. Drama.

Showtime ATL. Club Pyramids is da spot 2nite. If u ain't here u need to be.

I wonder how many people really think Dreya is writing these Twitter messages. The responses from her "fans" are crazy. People talking about how much they love her, guys posting their numbers for her to call. Crazy.

Sam and I called a couple of the numbers and had me pretend to be Dreya. It was funny as what. One of the guys was somebody from our school. I went off on him, saying he should be ashamed because he knows he's got a girlfriend. If his girl only knew!

I hear Sam's track blasting through the speakers and see Truth take the stage. He looks extra shiny in his wifebeater, like he's rubbed baby oil all over his arms. It makes him look even more cut up than usual, and it makes the shirt stick to his torso. The women are hollering in delight, like he's not nineteen.

Dreya sashays out with a microphone in her hand. She says, "Y'all ready to party with my man, Truth?"

The crowd hollers back at her. She grins and sings the hook to the song. While she's singing she ignores the choreographed moves of the dancers and does her own moves. She's got the guys pumped by how she dips to the floor and pops her booty on the way back up.

How could she not be embarrassed to dance like that with Aunt Charlie in the audience? My mama is never gonna see me doing stripper moves on the stage. No, ma'am.

When they get through with "What Ya Gonna Do," Truth launches into a few more tracks off his album. He's really good, and energetic. He's got the crowd eating out of the palm of his hand.

Since Dreya's not on any of his other songs, she doesn't really need to be out on the stage still, but she stays for the whole set, entertaining the crowd with her gyrations. When they finally leave the stage, they get a thunderous round of applause before the DJ takes over.

Backstage, Big D pops a bottle of champagne. "Y'all ripped it up out there! If y'all can make it in Atlanta, then every other city will be cake! This was the test."

"It was hot, wasn't it?" Dreya asks.

Big D kisses Dreya on her sweaty forehead. "Drama, baby, they were eating you up! You didn't tell me you could move like that, girl! You didn't do any of that in rehearsal."

"I guess I feed off the crowd," she replies. "They were getting me pumped, so I just put my back into it."

Truth says, "I thought I was gonna have to off somebody the way you had them dudes drooling, baby. You were on fire."

Big D says, "The tour bus is waiting outside. We're leaving for Birmingham in a few. Take a quick shower here and be on the bus in twenty minutes."

"Bethany, you staying here to help Dreya?" I ask.

"Yes, of course. Drama, what do you need?"

"Can you just put away all of my stuff and please bring my clothes to me so I can change in the shower area?"

"Yes, Drama. I've got it covered."

I'm tripping that I heard Dreya say please. She must be happy from having a good performance, because she's given her evil persona a take five. I hope she keeps that evil heifer in the bag until we get off the tour bus at the hotel in Birmingham, because I'm not trying to deal with her.

Sam and I go outside to get settled on the bus. He's already claimed our seat near the back, so we can collaborate and chill without being bothered. Truth and Drama have separate, extra large areas at the back of the bus with full beds, while the rest of us have to try to catch our shut-eye in the bus seats.

"Did you like the show?" he asks me, once we get settled in our seats.

"Well, I thought Truth did a great job, but I could barely hear Dreya's vocals over the track."

"Yeah, her voice doesn't really carry far. And I don't know why she thinks she has to dance all hard like that. She doesn't have the wind to dance and sing at the same time. It looked hot, but she sounded a mess."

"See, I wasn't even gonna say anything, because I thought they would say I was hating. But her vocals sounded crazy to me. I'm glad I'm not the only one who thought that."

"I'm gonna talk to Big D about it and see if he wants you to back Dreya up on stage. Actually, you and Bethany can be out there like backup singers, but Bethany can just lip-synch. Then it won't be too obvious that your voice is helping Dreya."

"We don't have anything to wear on stage, though."

"Most of these shows are in malls. Your jeans and baby tees should be good enough. I'm especially worried about *106 & Park,* though. That's going to be televised, and Dreya can't be on there sounding like a wounded raccoon."

"What do you think Big D will say?"

"He'll agree, but you'll have to go shopping in New York. You've gotta wear something fly on the show."

I'm down with this, but why does Bethany have to get a chance to shine, too? I know Dreya only invited her on this tour to make me mad. Dreya can't even stand Bethany, and I'm starting to join that crowd. I can't believe we were ever besties.

One by one, everyone loads onto the bus. It's not a huge entourage, but several of Truth's homeboys are with us, a couple of Big D's associates, the makeup artist—who finally showed up—and a hairstylist. Dreya and Bethany get on the bus last, and Dreya looks tired as what. She's scrubbed off all her makeup and has her short do in a head wrap.

Aunt Charlie is with them, too. I hope she doesn't think she's going on tour with us. That is *not* what's up!

"Didn't my baby work it out?" Aunt Charlie asks no one in particular.

Since she doesn't get a response from the exhausted road crew, she gives one herself.

"Yeah, Drama, girl, you are the stuff! You 'bout to make this paper!"

Dreya gives her mother a weak smile. "I know that's right, Ma."

Aunt Charlie turns toward me. "Sunday, you watch and learn boo. Let Dreya show you what Tollivers are made of. Y'all be cool on this tour. Don't make me have to bail nobody out!"

I roll my eyes extra hard as Aunt Charlie bounces, bobs, and dances off the bus.

"Where is my bed?" Dreya asks wearily.

Bethany shows her to the back of the bus and even throws the covers back for Dreya to get in.

Sam elbows me. "Looks like somebody is trying to steal your job."

"Yeah. She'll eventually do something to get on Dreya's nerves, though. They can't stand each other."

"So why did Dreya ask her to come on the tour?"

"To get back at me. She thinks Truth wants me, just because he gave me a ride in his new car."

"For real? When did that happen?"

Dang. Me and my loose lips. I forgot that I didn't mention that to Sam.

"I don't know. I think it was the day you took me to the aquarium."

Sam nods. "Wow. You conveniently forgot to tell me about that one. Wonder why?"

"Because it wasn't important."

"Yeah, I guess. Wake me up when we get to Birmingham."

Sam leans his chair back and closes his eyes. I can't figure out if he's mad at me or not. Maybe I should've told him about Truth trying to push up on me. Now it seems too late to make that revelation without him thinking I was feeling some kind of way about Truth.

Truth and his boys are drinking champagne and chilling loudly, near the middle section of the bus. It doesn't look like Truth showered or changed clothes, because he's still wearing that greasy-looking wifebeater.

Bethany finishes tucking Dreya in and takes her seat right in the center of Truth and his boys. She's already picked which one of Truth's entourage she wants to get cozy with for the tour. Honestly, I don't care which one she picks as long as she's not in Sam's face.

"Hey, Sunday," Truth yells. "What did you think about the show?"

"It was hot," I yell back. "You did a good set."

"Now see, I believe it when she says it, because Sunday is real. The rest of y'all some groupies."

Uh-oh. I think Truth drank a little bit too much truth serum.

"That's a real chick right there." Truth slurs some of his words as he points in my direction. "And she can blow, too. She can out sing my baby, but she ain't fly like Drama."

Big D pulls Truth's shirt and makes him sit down. "Man, close your eyes and get some rest. You've got five cities to go. Save all that for after the tour."

And with that it was lights-out for everybody on the bus, including Truth. Since I'm not tired, I turn on my iPod and listen to a few of Mystique's songs. I can't wait until New York, so I can meet her and get my big break. This assistant/groupie stuff is for the birds.

Plus, if I don't get away from Truth and Dreya soon, I think something is gonna end up popping off. But my meeting with Mystique is only a few days away. We can hold it together for that long, right?

21

Dreya's entire staff is piled into her Birmingham hotel suite, helping her get ready for the mall concert that happens in an hour. The hairstylist did something new with her short do. It's curled in hundreds of miniature spirals. Very cute.

The makeup artist is working on her now. She's spraying foundation onto her face from what looks like a spray-paint can. I've provided the twelve-pack of Sprite, which was a pain, because the only store I had access to was the gas station store, which didn't have twelve-packs. So I had to buy twelve separate cans of Sprite. Aaarrggh!

Get this, though. Bethany is rubbing Dreya's feet. She's got a big bottle of oil, has lit some aromatherapy candles, and is giving Dreya a foot rub. If that's what it takes to be Dreya's perfect assistant, Bethany can have that job. I'm not rubbing on anybody's feet. Especially not Dreya's evil self.

There's a knock on the door. I open the door and it's Sam.

"I'm not fully dressed!" Dreya shouts. "Don't let none of them hardheads in here!"

I step out into the hallway and give Sam a hug. "Did you sleep well?"

"Yeah, I did. How about you?"

"Bethany was on the phone half the night, but I finally did fall asleep."

"Who was she talking to?"

"Her friends back home. Bragging about the tour, being on the tour bus, all that."

"Did she brag about rubbing on Dreya's crusty feet?"

"I know, right? Probably not. She's taking this assistant job to the extreme."

"So, I mentioned to Big D about you and Bethany singing backup for Dreya."

"And?"

"He wanted to give Dreya another chance at the mall today before we implement that. He says the club was noisy last night, and that it was her first time out. He wants her to get the hang of how to project her voice on stage."

"Okay. It's cool. We'll see what happens."

"Make sure everyone's luggage is in the hallway. We leave for Orlando as soon as the mall show is over. It's an eight-hour drive."

"Okay."

I go back into the room, and Bethany is still rubbing on Dreya.

"Bethany, why don't you get up and help get Dreya's stuff together. They want to pack the bus up, and she'll be mad if any of her stuff gets left behind."

Bethany looks up at Dreya as if for approval. Dreya gives her a slight nod and waves her hand.

Bethany jumps up and starts looking around the room to compile all of Dreya's shoes, clothes, toiletries, and everything else. She scurries around the room like an Oompa-Loompa at Willy Wonka's chocolate factory. I'm in chill mode, moving briskly, but cool at the same time.

The makeup artist turns Dreya around to the mirror to view the finished product. That girl has done wonders on Dreya's acne-prone skin. I can't see a blackhead, blemish, pimple, or freckle—just a layer of bronze makeup.

"You look good," I comment.

"I do, don't I?" Dreya replies.

I shake my head and toss a pair of flip-flops from underneath the bed into Dreya's suitcase. I mean, could she try to be a little bit modest?

A little later, we're all on the bus and on our way to the mall. I don't know how much promotion they've done for this tour, but I blasted it to all of Dreya's Twitter followers (which have grown to over four thousand in a week) and to her Facebook fan group.

Sam handles Truth's Twitter account, which is even funnier than Dreya's. I can't even count the number of direct messages Truth has received that include pictures of half-naked (and all the way naked) teenage girls. Digital cameras take groupies to a whole other level.

On the way to the mall, I get a phone call from my mother. "Hi, Mommy."

"Hey, Sunday. Is everything going okay on the tour so far? Is everyone behaving?"

"Yes, Mom. Everyone is behaving. How are you doing? You sound sad."

"It's nothing. I don't want to worry you with it right now. I want you to have fun."

"Mommy, you know I'm not gonna have fun if I think you're at home sad about something."

"Honey, it's nothing you can help with. I just miss Carlos. Not hearing from him is torture."

"If he's hiding out, he'll get word to you soon, I'm sure."

"Just have fun, baby, and don't let Dreya steal your joy."

I give a soft chuckle. "I won't let her steal it. She's too busy stealing Bethany's joy."

"That poor girl! She wants to be rich and famous so badly."

"Mommy, she rubs Dreya's feet!"

Now I hear my mother laughing. "What? Dreya is out of control! Just a few weeks ago she was getting peed on by Manny in the middle of the night, and now she's got people rubbing on her feet?"

"Not people. Just Bethany."

"How's my future son-in-law?" my mother asks. I know she's talking about Sam.

"Why are you trying to marry me off? I haven't even graduated from high school yet."

"I know. I just really like him. He's a nice guy."

"I like him, too, but I ain't trying to marry the dude!"

Again I hear my mother laugh. Music to my ears.

"Okay, sweetie. Call me if you need anything."

"I will. Bye!"

I press End on my phone and Sam is staring at me. "What?"

"Who were you talking about at the end? Who do you like?"

I give him a tight frown. "Dang, you nosy. Why you all up in mine?"

"Were you talking about me or Truth?"

I laugh out loud. "What are you tripping on, boy?"

"Nothing."

When we get to the mall, there's no dressing room or backstage area. Just a platform in the middle of the mall, a CD player for the track and a few microphones. A step down from the club, but cool nonetheless. The show is about to start in a few minutes, and a small crowd of teenagers has started to form around the stage.

"I love you, Truth!" a young girl screams up at the stage.

"I love you, too, baby!" he yells back.

Sam, Big D, and I crack up laughing at the look on Dreya's face. She looks ready to jump off the stage and punch that poor little girl out. Instead, she does her microphone sound check with a frown on her face.

Big D says, "She better get used to groupies. It hasn't even started yet!"

By the time we're ready to start the show, there's about fifty people standing near the stage. Only fifty people showed up for a free concert? It's a good thing they didn't charge admission.

They kick off the show with Truth's album tracks, and close it out with "What Ya Gonna Do." The small crowd is energetic to say the least. What they don't have in numbers, they make up for with the handful of screaming teenagers who can't seem to get enough of Truth, his long locs, and his skintight tank top.

Truth yells to the crowd, "Thank you, Birmingham! Don't forget to cop that album. It'll be in stores soon."

The tiny crowd disperses, and Dreya just stands on the stage looking dumbfounded, like she can't believe she just did a concert for a handful of people.

Big D says, "All right, y'all. We're gonna hit the food court and then we're right back on the road. We've got an eight-hour drive to Orlando."

Dreya asks, "Where in the world is everybody? Did they not know we were coming?"

"It's a holiday, sweetie," Big D says. "Everyone's at home about to grub on turkey. The mall closes early today, so hurry up and get yourself something to eat."

Dreya walks down the platform stairs in a daze. Bethany is waiting at the bottom of the stairs to collect her.

"Come on," Bethany says, "I'll get you some Panda Express."

As they walk away, Sam and I burst into laughter. "Oh, my goodness, did you see her face?" I ask.

"The diva is looking throwed right now! She's tripping that nobody came checking for her."

I say, "She needed that, though, because her head was way too big. Got people rubbing her feet like she's a platinum-selling artist already."

"I'm still laughing at how she looked at that little girl from the stage," Sam adds. "That poor little girl was about to get stole on."

"I know! What's the itinerary for Orlando? Is it another mall show?"

"We're actually there for two days. We'll get there tonight and then tomorrow is the show. And yeah, it's another mall show. The bus will pull off the next morning on the way to Charlotte, which is a nine-hour drive."

"Yikes—nine hours? Will they have to perform that night?"

"Yep, at the local radio station's Turkey Jam. It's a free concert, but there should be a big crowd, because they've got some headliners on the roster."

"What kind of headliners?" I ask. "Is Mystique gonna be there?"

Sam laughs out loud. "Nah, she doesn't do free concerts. Ginuwine is the headliner."

"Ginuwine! He's like forty years old, right?"

"I don't know if he's that old, but the ladies still come out to see him!"

"That's an older crowd, though. Will they be feeling Dreya and Truth?"

"I don't know. We'll see. A gig is a gig."

Big D directs the crew to grab all of their stuff from the stage and head back to the bus. Instead of using the stairs, he jumps off the stage and lands in front of me and Sam. "What did y'all think?"

"It was cool," Sam says. "I don't think Drama can handle the low attendance."

Big D laughs out loud. "She'll get used to it. It's part of the game."

"But what about what we discussed—with Sunday backing her up?" Sam asks.

"We're gonna implement that at the Turkey Jam."

"What if Dreya doesn't want to do it?" I ask.

Big D replies, "It's not her decision. She's just gonna have to get over it. Y'all need to get something to eat. We need to be on the bus in an hour."

Sam and I head up to the food court, and we notice a small crowd around the Panda Express. Truth and Dreya have been mobbed by a group of teenagers wanting autographs. Dreya beams happily as she signs the little slips of paper and flyers from the record store.

"It's a good thing she got mobbed like this. I sure didn't want to be on the bus with her for eight hours in a foul mood," I say to Sam.

"Right. Let's get some McDonald's. You want your dollar-menu special?"

"You know it!" I say.

"Oh, I almost forgot," Sam says. "I bought you something before the show started."

My eyes light up. "What did you get me?"

"It's nothing, really." He fishes in his pocket and pulls out a box from Claire's.

I take it from his hands with a smile. "Thank you!"

Inside the box is a silver charm bracelet with one charm. It has the letter *S* dangling from it with a small pink crystal in the middle of the letter.

"It's not real or anything. I just thought it was cute, and it has my initial."

"I noticed that. But it's my initial, too. So will anybody get the message?"

He shrugs. "As long as you know what it means. You're my girl, so Truth can step."

"I'm *your* girl? Is that a request or a demand?"

"I thought you wanted to be my girl. I'm just giving you what you want."

"It's not that I'm not feeling you, because I am. But I want to get this paper right now. College is calling my name."

"You can't get this money and be my girl?"

"Maybe . . . but do I have to decide right now?"

Sam frowns. "Why not? Do you want to still give Truth a chance?"

"Dead that. I ain't thinking about him."

I clip on the bracelet and smile up at Sam. "I like this. Thank you."

"Well, just like I'm planning to take you to a real dinner when we blow up, I'll buy you some real jewelry, too."

"Okay. I'm gonna hold you to that. Every girl likes diamonds."

"Even you? I thought you weren't a girly girl."

"I'm not, but I like diamonds!"

"Okay, so when we blow up, I'm gonna ice you all the way out!"

I give Sam a hug. Not an "I'm your girlfriend" kind of hug, but a hug that says, "I'm your friend." He takes it, I guess, because he knows that's all I'm offering to him right now.

I've got my mind on a come-up, and even though Sam has this crush thing happening, his mind is on a come-up, too.

I love how he says *when* we blow up instead of *if* we blow up! I mean, you can't achieve something if you don't believe it!

And trust, I believe it.

22

I'm glad I thought to pack my swimsuit, because it's still warm when we make it into Orlando. Plus, our hotel has a heated indoor pool. Everyone agrees that a pool party is exactly what we need to unwind from being on the road all day.

Bethany and I silently change in our hotel room. We haven't really had any conversation on this tour so far. I'm irritated that she's even here, so I really don't feel the need to irritate myself further by talking to her.

"So we aren't friends anymore?" Bethany asks.

"Girl, please. After what you did with Romell, I can't even believe you're asking me that."

"You and Romell weren't even together. Why do you care if I talked to him?"

"I don't care that you talked to him, but the reason why you talked to him is what made us not be friends."

Bethany slides a swimsuit cover-up over her head. It's

not really covering anything up because it's sheer and clingy, but I'm sure that's the effect that she was going for.

"Oh, really?" Bethany asks. "The reason I talked to Romell is because I've always liked him, even before you two got together."

"Whatever, Bethany."

"You always want to say whatever when you're the one in the wrong. You knew that I liked him and then you stole him for yourself. Like you do with all the boys."

I roll my eyes. "Bethany, look, I don't care. I'm not on that anymore with you. You and Dreya can be friends if you want to, but you and I are not."

"What about Daddy's Little Girls?"

I laugh out loud. "If you hadn't already noticed, the group has been disbanded. There is no more Daddy's Little Girls."

"So just like that, you're giving up on our dreams? What about the red carpets, traveling all over the world doing concerts, the Grammys and all that?"

"Those were your dreams, Bethany. I'm not stopping you from achieving any of that. Why don't you talk to Big D about getting yourself a record deal? The industry could always use another Britney Spears. Lord knows, you're a train wreck waiting to happen."

"When did you get to be so mean, Sunday? We've been best friends since we were little."

"Since your hormones kicked in and you went boy crazy, that's when. Do me a favor and leave me alone on this tour, Bethany."

I grab my pool towel and storm out of the room. I meet Sam, Truth, and a few other guys at the elevator.

"Where's the rest of the girls?" Truth asks.

"I don't know. They're coming, I guess."

One of Truth's homeboys looks me up and down. "Have we met? I'm Chauncey."

"Yes, we have met. Several times! I'm Sunday, remember . . . ?"

"Oh, right. You're Sam's girl."

I lift an eyebrow at Sam, and he looks at his feet. Sounds like he's been running his mouth.

"Sam and I are cool. . . ." I decide not to put him on blast, but he's gonna feel the pain later. I do not roll like this!

All the guys burst out laughing and give Sam fist pounds and chest bumps. Sam is blushing a little bit, but managing to look hard at the same time.

"Man, if a square like you can pull a hottie like this," Chauncey says, "it must be a shortage of black dudes."

"Yeah, most of y'all too busy chasing beckys," Bethany says as she sashays to the front of the group, giving all the boys a view of her bottom.

Chauncey high-fives a few other dudes. "That's what I'm talking 'bout."

As Bethany walks by, I see that her face is streaked with tears. What does she have to cry about? I find myself feeling a little bit sad that we're not friends anymore, but not enough to make me shed any tears. She brought it on herself anyway.

When we get to the pool, Dreya; her makeup artist,

Regina; and the hairstylist, Monie, are already there, lounging on the pool chairs.

"Don't even think about doing no cannonballs by me!" Dreya shouts at the boys. "I am not trying to get my hair wet."

"How you gonna come to the pool and expect to stay dry?" Truth asks. "You shoulda stayed in the room."

Dreya rolls her eyes. "That's what you wanted, right? For me to stay upstairs so you could get your flirt on?"

"Who am I flirting with?" Truth asks.

"Anyone? How about that fourteen-year-old at the mall? How about her?"

Truth laughs and splashes water over in Dreya's direction. "You're not serious, are you? That was a fan. Did you see me getting mad when you were shaking your booty in front of all those guys at Club Pyramids? Shoot, I shoulda been mad, seeing that we knew half the people in the crowd!"

Dreya rolls her eyes. "Whatever! I was performing. I didn't tell any of them that I loved them."

Sam yells, "Can y'all chill with that? I know your name is Drama, but dang, can the rest of us get a vacation?"

Everyone bursts into a flurry of laughter and splashes. I guess everyone is tired of Dreya and her mess, not just me. Before I get into the pool, I take a few pictures of everyone with my digital camera. Later, I'll upload them to Twitter. The girls will like these shirtless photos of Truth, and Dreya sitting by the pool looking stank. I deliberately don't take any pictures of Bethany. I refuse to give her any publicity at all.

After I'm done with the pictures, I take a flying leap into the pool. I come up from the water, right in front of Truth. He takes this as his opportunity and lifts me up by my legs and tosses me.

Sam doesn't look too thrilled when I finally pop up from underneath the water, but he doesn't say anything. I quickly swim away from Truth before he touches me again. Number one, I don't like being dunked, and number two, I swear he tried to get a free feel.

"You running, Sunday?" Truth yells. "You a sucka!"

Nobody laughs at this, probably because they see what I see. Sam is sneaking up behind Truth. Before Truth realizes Sam is back there, Sam lifts Truth into the air and slams him head first into the water.

Truth comes back up with a quickness. "It's on now!"

Truth chases Sam through the water and tries to dunk him, but he can't get the job done. So some of Truth's boys help him, and they all slam Sam into the water.

"Get off of him!" I scream from my safe position outside of the pool.

When Sam comes up for air, everyone is laughing and having a good time. Everyone except Dreya, who, in the crossfire, got completely drenched.

"I told y'all not to get my hair wet!" she screams.

Truth lifts his eyebrows over in Dreya's direction. "Well, y'all, she is already wet."

As if on cue, all the boys jump out of the pool and run toward Dreya. The hairstylist and makeup artist get away, but Dreya isn't fast enough. They all lift her in the air like a bunch of men carrying a queen through the village. Except they aren't taking her to somewhere glorious, they're body-slamming her in some chlorine-filled water.

Dreya comes up sputtering and mad! "I hate y'all!" she yells.

Everyone stands there quietly, waiting to see what else Dreya will do. But she looks down and sees her evil-looking reflection in the water and bursts out laughing. We join her in laughing, because she really does look ridiculous.

"I still hate y'all," she says between snorts.

"But we all love you, Drama." Truth jumps in the water, scoops Dreya into his arms, and gives her a kiss.

23

I think everybody needed the break we got at our pool party. The Orlando show went much better than the Birmingham show. There were about two hundred teenagers in the crowd and they were screaming their heads off for Truth and Drama.

Everybody kind of crashed back at the hotel. We didn't do much partying, because we have a long ride today. We've got nine hours until we get to Charlotte.

"Hey!" Bethany yells as the bus pulls out of the hotel parking lot. "There are pictures from the Atlanta show up on Sandrarose.com!"

Sandra Rose is like one of the top gossip mavens in Atlanta! Anything that goes down in the A, she knows about it, and she is quick to put a celebrity on blast. The stars take off running when they see Sandra with that camera around her neck. I'm surprised that she's putting something up about Truth and Dreya already. They're newcomers to the game and she usually doesn't give too much press to any up-and-comers.

Dreya squeals, "Let me see! What does the article say?"

Bethany reads out loud. "Atlanta artists Truth and Drama gave a concert at Club Pyramids on Thanksgiving night. There's a lot of buzz about this new duo, and their song sounds like a hit. But sources tell me that the romance is manufactured and that Truth is really more interested in Drama's cousin and assistant, Sunday. The last pic in this spread just might prove this rumor to be true. Time will tell."

"What!" Dreya screams. "Let me see the picture."

I pull up Sandrarose.com on my own phone so that I can see for myself. The picture is completely innocent, I think. I'm standing in the hallway behind the dressing room, doing something with my phone. Oh, that's when I was putting up Dreya's Twitter messages. Truth is standing behind me, and he seems to be staring at my booty, and he's biting his bottom lip.

Dreya throws Bethany's phone at Truth and storms to the back of the bus. He laughs, picks up the phone, and looks at the picture. Then he laughs some more.

"Dreya, stop tripping! I wasn't even thinking about Sunday! I was practicing my lyrics in my head. I don't even think I knew she was out there!"

"So what!" Dreya yells. "Everyone thinks that you want her now! Everyone is laughing at me."

"Do you think people believe half the stuff Sandra

Rose says? She gets her stories from *sources*. Come on now! I bet some of the stuff she just makes up off the top of her head."

I don't say anything, because I don't want to be in the middle of their argument. But I read Sandra Rose all the time, and for the most part her stuff is accurate. Every now and then she gets it wrong, but usually she's right on target. I wonder who her source was on this story.

Sam's face is real tight. "You okay?" I ask.

"Yeah, I'm good. I just feel like I'm getting played sometimes."

"By who? Not by me, I hope? I'm not thinking about Truth."

He shrugs. "I don't know. I just feel played."

"Well, what do you mean? Tell me what you mean."

"Come on, Sunday. Truth is staring at you in that picture like he wants to get it in."

"You saw the blog post?"

"Yeah, I saw it. Truth thinks he can have it all. Record deal, Drama, and you, too?"

"He doesn't have me."

"Right. You keep saying that. But you sure are hesitating about being my girl, like you're waiting for something else to pop off."

"You're tripping, Sam, you know that—right?"

"Whatever."

It's a tense nine hours to Charlotte. Dreya stays in her secluded area the whole time, sometimes crying, sometimes yelling at Truth. Big D can't even calm her down by telling her that all of it is publicity that will help blow up her album sales.

By the time we get to Charlotte, Dreya's voice is hoarse from all of the crying and hollering she's done on the bus. Sam doesn't even sit next to me on the bus. He goes to the front with the crew and pretends that he needs to talk about stage logistics and whatnot. He's mad, too, but for totally no reason. I don't know how many times I have to say the same thing before he's convinced.

It's five o'clock now and the show is at seven, in a teen nightclub. When we get to the hotel, Bethany tries making Dreya some tea, but she refuses to drink it.

Big D bursts into Dreya's hotel room and says, "Drama, you need to get that tea down your throat. The show is in less than two hours. I need you to get your voice right."

"No. They're not going to make fun of me," Dreya whispers. "Let them see what they'll do without Drama."

Big D looks like he's about to blow up. "Sunday, put on the flyest outfit you have. You're gonna perform in Drama's place tonight."

"No, she isn't! She can't replace me!" Dreya squeaks.

"I told you to stop tripping about that blogger, but you wanted to act a fool," Big D says. "Now you've lost your voice. I've got paper to stack, and that means the show must go on."

"But I don't know the choreography," I say, trying to think of anything that will get me off the hook.

Big D shrugs. "Neither does Dreya. You can do whatever you want to do out there—just sing that hook."

I take one look at Dreya before I leave the room, and

she is throwing me some serious evil eye. She can't be mad at me, though. It's her own fault. She knows that I don't want Truth, so that blog article shouldn't have even bothered her.

I go up to my room and pull out the cutest outfit I have. A jean skirt, baby tee, and some Ugg boots. It's not like Drama's style, but it'll have to do.

There's a knock on my hotel room door. I open it to Monie and Regina, Dreya's hairstylist and makeup artist.

"What's going on?" I ask.

"Big D said to come up here and hook you up," Monie says.

"But won't Dreya be mad?"

Regina shrugs. "Big D is the one who cuts our checks, so we do what he says."

Monie pulls the ponytail holder out of my hair. "Now what are we gonna do with this?"

In less than an hour, Monie and Regina have me looking like true diva material. I've never been so gelled, glossy, and glittery in my life.

"This girl is a masterpiece!" Regina says.

"You got that right," Monie replies with a giggle. "If Truth didn't want her before, he might be checking for her now."

"Y'all stop that," I say. "That's what started all this mess to begin with."

"Sorry," Regina says. "We just think it's cute that y'all got a little teenage love triangle going on."

"We don't!" I say.

They leave, but they're giggling the entire way down

the hall. I don't think they believe a word I'm saying about not liking Truth.

When I hear a knock on my door, I think it's them coming back. I swing it open to fuss some more, but it's Sam.

"Well, look at you. You look good, girl," he says.

At least he doesn't seem mad at me, nor is he making any jokes about Truth. "Regina and Monie threw something together, but it'll have to do."

"They did a good job, and so will you at the show. Good luck."

"Do you mean that? You aren't still mad about the Sandra Rose thing, are you?"

He shakes his head. "Nah. All of this is just gonna end up making you a star. And that's the goal, right?"

I nod. "Yeah, that's the goal."

I decide not to spend Truth's entire set out on the stage like Dreya does. They only need me on the one song, and I don't like the spotlight enough to stay out there the whole time. Luckily, we're doing "What Ya Gonna Do" first, so I can hurry up and get it over with.

I stand backstage until I get my cue. Dreya and Bethany stand behind me, both giving me evil glares. Dreya is finally sipping on her tea, but it's too late now. I think she's learned her lesson. Big D doesn't play.

"You're not gonna take my spot," Dreya hisses.

"I don't want your spot," I hiss back. "Plus, you've already signed a record deal. What are you worried about?"

"Just make sure you don't forget it."

I roll my eyes as the music comes on. Next I'm running

out on stage with Truth and doing my own little dance moves. They are nowhere near as seductive as Dreya's, but that's not my style.

I get pumped that the audience knows the words to the hook and they're singing with me. This is my music they're getting pumped about, which, of course, makes me pumped, too!

At the end of the song, I jog off the stage, still feeling the rush of adrenaline pumping through my body.

"You did great," Big D says. "You were getting them hyped out there."

"I wasn't doing all that booty popping like Dreya does, though."

"That's unnecessary, and it's her, not you. You did fine. I bet she'll get that voice in order now, won't she?"

I laugh. "Yeah, she will. She thinks I'm trying to take her place."

Big D replies, "A little healthy competition ain't ever hurt nobody."

24

The stops in Chicago, Detroit, and Boston were all the same. Cold! I'm so glad to live in Atlanta that I don't know what to do. Dreya made sure she got her voice together and she sang and danced her butt off in all three cities. She and Truth made up, too, because Sandra Rose printed something else about them that was more favorable to Dreya. Sandra even called Dreya a goddess. I'm not sure what she meant by that, but hey, it made Dreya happy again.

That's a good thing, because Dreya being hateful was making the tour the opposite of fun. Bethany took the brunt of her anger, though, and had to do all kinds of ridiculous errands. It's almost a shame that Bethany isn't getting a dime for being on this tour with us. She's just rolling groupie-style, wishing, hoping, and praying for a come-up of her own.

But now we're at the last city on the tour. New York,

baby! At the courtesy of BET and Mystique, we're staying at the Ritz-Carlton, and we'll be in the city for three whole days. Dreya and Truth have to do some radio interviews and contests to get people hyped about the episode of *106 & Park*.

I need to go shopping, because Big D told me and Bethany to look hot. We're going on stage with Dreya and Truth. He doesn't want to take a chance of Dreya's voice giving out on her because she's been singing all week.

Monie and Regina take me to Barneys. I don't have Barneys money, but Big D gave me a credit card and told me to listen to Monie and Regina. I'm thinking that one of them must be Big D's woman on the side, because it is kind of odd that Shelly isn't on this trip.

When we get to Barneys, Regina drags me to the junior section. In minutes they've put together a Juicy Couture ensemble. It's a pink half sweater, gray wool skirt, and sparkly pink tights. Then they find some designer boots that have an ungodly price tag.

"At least they're not Louboutins," Regina says. "They're pretty reasonable, actually."

"I guess. If six hundred dollars is reasonable," I say.

"Trust me, these are the cheapest boots in the store," Monie adds.

"I've got to hurry, y'all. Big D set up a meeting this afternoon for me, Sam, and Mystique."

Regina says, "Well, let's get you out of here. We've got to get you fly for that meeting!"

I meet Sam and Big D in the hotel lobby at 12:45 p.m. sharp. Our meeting is scheduled for 1:15 p.m. in the hotel restaurant, although Big D doesn't expect Mystique to show up until 2:00 p.m. Stars never show up on time.

"You've got the music, right?" I ask Sam.

He smiles and holds up an MP3 player, an iPod Shuffle, and a CD. "I've got every listening medium. She said she wanted to take a listen at lunch."

"I'm nervous! What if she doesn't like it?" I ask.

My nerves are shot, thinking about how Mystique is going to react to my music. I didn't start getting nervous until I let Regina and Monie help me get dressed. They kept talking about how this is my big break and how I can't afford to mess this up.

They got all the way inside my head and made little butterflies dance a jig in my stomach.

"She'll love it," Big D says. "Trust me when I say, that track sounds like something Ne-Yo did."

"I love Ne-Yo!" I exclaim.

"Well, it's just that original and current. Relax, she's going to want you on her team. Spelman, here you come!"

After Big D's pep talk, I'm a little bit calmer, but I still feel my leg shaking under the table.

Mystique surprises us by showing up right after we sit down! She's not only on time, but early. It's only one o'clock! Her bodyguard walks her into the restaurant and stands behind her, looking like a WWE wrestler in a suit.

The hostess leads them over to our table; Big D and Sam stand up. I can't decide if I should or not, so I just stay seated.

"I'm Mystique." She shakes hands with Big D and Sam and gives me a hug.

Her bodyguard takes a seat at the table behind us. I guess he's trying to give us our privacy, but he's totally there, hulking in the background. I try to ignore him, but I can hear him breathing and his fingers drumming on the table.

Big D says, "You already know me, and these are my songwriting geniuses Sam Wilkins and Sunday Tolliver."

"It's so good to see you, Deionte, and meet you, Sam and Sunday. I know I'm a little early for our meeting, but I really want to hear this song!"

She pulls a set of earphones out of her purse. "Who has the song?"

Sam fumbles with the iPod but hooks her earphones up to it and flicks to our song. She closes her eyes while she listens. Her face shows no emotion, but her head bobs up and down in time with the music. I think she's enjoying it, but I can't tell.

When the song finishes she says, "Let me hear it one more time."

A huge smile crosses Big D's face. Her wanting to hear it again must be a good sign! Sam presses Play once more, and this time she hums along on some parts, sings on others, and hits a few ad-libs. She's freaking the song and making it her own! OMG! She likes it!

At the end of the second play she says, "I have to have this song on my new album. It's a single, too, I can tell."

Sam and I just stare, both of us without words! Big D lets out a huge laugh.

"I think they weren't expecting you to love it," he says. "Both of them look like they're in a state of shock."

"I . . . I'm honored," I stammer. "That would be a dream come true for you to sing this song."

"You guys don't have a name yet, so I'll pay fifty thousand on the front end. But you'll get songwriter credit and points, too."

I look at Big D and hope he can read my mind. "Points are how they calculate royalties. This is a huge break for y'all, because, like I said, most new songwriters don't get points."

"I heard someone was trying to pay for college," Mystique says. "I hope you get into Spelman, Sunday, and I wish you the best. I always wanted to go to college myself, but I started in this industry when I was nine years old."

Can I just say that I can't believe she's this nice! She has sold millions of records worldwide, has Grammys, AMAs, VMAs, and every other award you can think of, but she's sweet as pie. She keeps smiling at us with those beautifully whitened teeth!

Sam still hasn't said anything. "Mystique. Thank you," he croaks.

"Who's singing on the track?" Mystique asks. "Epsilon is giving me my own label and I'm looking for artists. That's not Drama, is it?"

"That's Sunday," Big D beams.

"Your voice is phenomenal, and you're beautiful, too," Mystique says. "Do you think you'd like to be on my label?"

I pause for a moment before answering. If I sign a record deal with Mystique, it would mean all of the things I'm doing right now: touring nonstop, shows, interviews, and constant traveling. How does this fit in with college?

"I know what you're thinking," Mystique says. "And we can work around school."

"But how? This tour stuff is already cutting into my school attendance."

"We could work it out if we tried really hard over the summer, and you could still attend Spelman in the fall. It would actually look good to sponsors that you are taking your education seriously."

"Can I think about it?" I ask.

Big D says, "Girl, this is a once-in-a-lifetime opportunity. You can't sleep on this."

Mystique lifts one hand. "No, Deionte, let her think about it. Her talent isn't going anywhere and neither is my offer. College is important and I'm betting that it's been her dream for a long time."

"It has been."

She reaches over the table and strokes my arm. "Well, dreams are something that I hold dear. Take all the time you need."

"Okay."

"I'll have my lawyers draw up some paperwork regarding this song."

"I'm sure your parents would want to look it over."

"Mine definitely will," I say.

Sam nods. "My mom will, too."

"We'll talk more after the *106 & Park* shooting. I need to take a nap before that. All those screaming kids are gonna give me a headache. Do y'all mind if I skip lunch?"

"No, of course not," Big D says. "Get your beauty rest—not that you need it."

She smiles and stands up, causing Sam and Big D to rise to their feet as well. This time I stand, too, because I want to give her a real hug if she tries to get one.

And she does!

When she leaves the restaurant and we all sit back down I say, "It feels like that happened too quickly. What am I missing?"

"Nothing," Big D says. "That's how it goes down in this industry. When opportunity knocks, you've got to be ready. It just so happened that you two were prepared with a hot song."

"But fifty thousand dollars? Just like that?" Sam asks. "That seems too good to be true."

"That girl is worth hundreds of millions of dollars, and the budget for her album is about ten million dollars. She got this song at a discount, on the front end, but y'all are gonna clean up in royalties."

I narrow my eyes. "What about you, Big D? What's your cut gonna be? I know you didn't set this all up out of the kindness of your heart."

He laughs. "Because I set all this up, I'm acting as your manager, and that entitles me to fifteen percent of everything y'all make."

"That's cool," Sam says. "Most managers try to get twenty percent."

"Okay. I guess it's cool," I concur.

"Both of y'all mother's are going to have to sign those documents and send them back before any cash changes hands."

I know my mother will sign without a doubt. I'm just thankful that my first year at Spelman is paid for! Now, even if my guidance counselor can't get me any scholarships, I'm good to go.

"I wish you would reconsider Mystique's offer for a record deal. Shoot, if I had been thinking straight I woulda signed you instead of your cousin."

"Yeah, you called me Disney, remember?"

"Yeah, I remember that. Somehow I don't think I could've sold you to Epsilon. That was some divine intervention or something that got Mystique on your bandwagon, girl."

I laugh out loud. "I wouldn't say she's on my bandwagon."

"Maybe not, but she sees what I see. Your talent isn't going anywhere, but then neither is Spelman," Big D says.

"I know, Big D. I said I was gonna think about it."

Sam flags down a waitress. "I don't know about y'all, but I'm hungry. Who wants lunch?"

It's only been a few moments since this all went down, but already the decision is weighing heavily on my mind. Spelman or a record deal? I never thought I'd have to make a choice like this. I can't even decide if I want a boyfriend! How can anyone expect me to make the right call on this?

25

We decide not to tell anyone about our meeting with Mystique. First of all, because we don't want to give Dreya anything to get mad about. And yeah, even though this has absolutely nothing to do with her, she'll find a way to make it her issue and pitch a fit.

Behtany and I head over to Dreya's suite for Regina and Monie to do their magic on us. If I was cool with Bethany right now, I'd mention that she has on a really cute outfit, but since we're not cool, I'm not saying anything.

"How did your meeting go?" Regina asks.

Dang, dang, dang! Forgot that I told her and Monie about the meeting with Mystique. I've been slipping lately on keeping secrets and stuff. It's a good thing I don't lie, because I sure wouldn't be able to keep up with them.

"What meeting?" Bethany asks.

"It was nothing. Just about some music. A song that me and Sam worked on."

"Well, who was the meeting with?" Dreya asks.

"You're nosy! Dang! None of your business."

Dreya stands up from Monie's chair. She puts both hands on her hips and flips the plastic smock she's wearing. "What do you mean, none of my business? Did you have a meeting with my man or something?"

"What? No! Girl, you are tripping. Nobody wants Truth. Please get that through your head."

"Well, why is it that when I tried to find him this afternoon for lunch, he was missing in action? I couldn't find any of y'all either. Sunday, Sam, Big D, Bethany. It sounds like y'all are planning something behind my back."

Bethany's eyes drop to the floor. I know that look. I know it like I know the back of my hand. I can guess where Truth was when Dreya was looking for him. He was probably hemmed up somewhere with Bethany.

"Maybe they're planning a surprise party," Regina offers.

"Nah, I don't think that was it," Dreya says. "Somebody in here's been creeping."

"Well, it wasn't me," I say. "I was with Sam—you can ask him. I can't, however, speak for everyone in this room. I'm just sayin'."

Dreya laughs out loud. "She wouldn't dare! Bethany knows better than to cross me. Not only will I beat that tail, I will kick her off my staff so fast her head will spin."

"I haven't done anything," Bethany says. "Sunday is tripping."

Monie tugs on Dreya's smock. "Honey, you need to sit your little hyper behind back down in this chair so you can get ready for this show. You wanna be on *106 & Park* with a half-done hairdo?"

Dreya rolls her eyes at everyone and sits back down. I can almost see the wheels in her head spinning and trying to figure out what's really going down. I don't care how fast those little wheels spin, she'll never figure out who I met with this afternoon without someone telling her.

We're supposed to meet in the lobby of the hotel at 4:00 p.m. for the special *106 & Park* taping. BET is sending three limos over to the Ritz-Carlton to pick up all of the acts, so that we can arrive in style. This new artist showcase is the business.

Dreya and Truth are hugged up on one of the lobby couches. She must've confronted him yet again, and he's trying to console her. I wonder if he'd bother having her as a girlfriend if it wasn't connected with his music career.

When the limos arrive, Sam pulls my arm. "Don't go out yet. Let Dreya and Truth pick a limo first, so we can get in a different one."

"I feel you on that."

We watch Dreya and Truth get in the first limo with a few other people and we make our way over to the last one. A little-girl group climbs in right behind us. They're all dressed alike and have a fancy lady with them.

"What's the name of y'all group?" I ask.

"Sugar and Spice," the woman replies.

"Aww . . . they're cute."

One of the little girls looks me up and down. "And who are you supposed to be?"

"Okay, wow. I'm Sunday Tolliver."

"You an artist?" she asks.

"Not exactly. I'm a songwriter."

"Oh, she ain't no competition. We cool."

"Competition? This is a contest?"

The woman replies, "Apparently a rumor has been going across the Internet that Mystique is looking for talent to sign to her new label. We don't have a record deal yet, so we're hoping the rumor is true."

"Well, good luck, y'all. I hope y'all get it," Sam says in the voice that he uses for Manny.

"Who's he talking to?" the sassy little girl says. "We don't need luck. We're Sugar and Spice. Hit it, girls."

Those four little girls bust some harmonies that make Daddy's Little Girls sound like amateurs. They're right. They don't need luck, they just need someone like Mystique to hear them and give them an opportunity.

Before we even walk in the *106 & Park* studio, we can hear the screaming! There are teenagers lined up on the street behind a barricade. They must be the ones who didn't make it in for the taping. They must be here for Mystique, because all that screaming can't be for these newcomers.

We're all lined up backstage according to when we'll perform, and we're last! That means we're closing out the show, and I think that's a good thing. The best for last.

Everyone makes their bathroom runs, gets water, tea, or Sprite if you're Dreya, and makes it back to the line in a hurry. No one wants to miss their opportunity to be on BET. Bethany and I are tuned up and ready to sing, although I don't want to sing with her.

"Y'all better make sure to only hit the harmonies," Dreya says. "No runs, Sunday, and no high notes, Bethany."

"You sure? I can hit a Mariah Carey note right at the end of the song," Bethany says.

"If you do that, I will beat the crap out of you, right there on national television."

I burst out laughing. "You do that, you'll end up on Sandrarose.com, Mediatakeout.com, Bossip.com, theybf.com, and Crunktastical.net."

"Why do you even know all those Web sites?"

"You should! That's where they post photos of celebrities in compromising positions. You need to check on there and see if they have any pictures of Truth and a groupie."

Truth walks up. "What did I hear about Truth and a groupie? Where's the groupie? I love groupies."

Dreya elbows him. "Shut up, Truth."

One of the show's associate producers comes backstage to make everyone quiet down because the show is starting. Sugar and Spice is up first and they sing a cute little song. I wish I could see them performing, cause I know that little sassy one is hamming it up. The crowd really gives them a huge round of applause when they're done.

"They can blow. They're trying to get a record deal with Mystique," I whisper.

"Well, they should," Dreya replies.

The next few groups are just all right. None of them sang or rapped well enough for me to consider even buying their records. Even the crowd applause was lackluster. Mystique had to practically beg the crowd to show them some love.

It's finally our turn, and after so many bad performances, the crowd could be ready to throw tomatoes or ready to get on their feet. I hope they're ready to dance!

Truth comes out first in his signature greasy tank top. I wonder what he does to give all those shirts that look! The girls start screaming as soon as he hits the stage. The rest of us, including the dancers, all hit the stage when the music starts. There's not much room, but the dancers are professionals. They know how to work with the little bit of space they have.

Truth is extremely pumped in his delivery. He runs by the front row, touching girls' hands as Dreya sings the hook and we harmonize. Dreya sounds great, too. She's definitely not trying to let anybody take her spot, especially not me or Bethany.

After the song is over, mostly everyone in the crowd jumps up and cheers. Mystique laughs over her microphone, because she's trying to get them to calm down, but they won't!

"Looks like we've got a hit maker right here," she says

over the screaming, and sends the show to a commercial break.

Backstage, while everyone is hugging one another and yelling, Big D stands off to one side looking strange, with his hand covering his mouth.

I walk up to him and ask, "Are you okay?"

Now that I'm up close to him I can see that he has tears in his eyes.

"Yeah, I'm okay. It's just . . . man . . . I've worked my whole life for this, and it's all blowing up right now. I just feel ridiculously blessed right now, that God has sent you to me."

"Me?"

Big D laughs. "Yes, you, Sunday. It was your hook that made that song so hot. And that song is what has propelled Truth into the spotlight. You might not know it, lil' mama, but you've got the golden touch."

"Nuh-uh!" I say. "I'm just doing what I love!"

"Well, I'm not the only one who sees it. Mystique isn't going to stop until she has you on her label."

"I'm still not sure about all that. I want to finish high school first before I do this. Something tells me that if I sign a record deal, my life will never be normal again."

Big D laughs out loud. "I've got news for you. Did you hear that applause? Life as you know it has officially ceased!"

Bethany steps to me as soon as Big D is out of earshot. It seems like lately she just lurks in the shadows trying to see what she can see, like some kind of spy for Dreya.

"So Mystique wants you on her label?" she asks.

"You just dipping with no shame whatsoever. You just tacky," I respond.

As I turn to walk away from her, she continues: "I can see Dreya only thinking of herself when she got a record deal, because she's selfish like that. But how could you not tell Mystique about our group? How could you do that?"

I stop in my tracks and turn to face Bethany. "You can't be for real, Bethany. You've been beyond foul ever since this record deal stuff started. Kicking with my ex and whatnot. How can you expect me to be lookin' out for you?"

"You don't even like Romell anymore! Why do you care if we're together?"

"I don't care. I just know that your reasons for hollering at him are messed up. You only want to date him because he dated me. You need to really find your own identity."

Bethany's jaw drops like I just slapped her. "I can't believe I ever thought you were my best friend."

"Ditto. I can't believe it either."

"Dreya is right about you," Bethany hisses. "She says that you've got everybody fooled. Everyone thinks you're all good and smart and sweet, but you're faker than fake."

I burst into a flurry of laughter. "Dreya calling somebody fake is like McDonald's claiming to have gourmet food. Unbelievable."

"You are a fake, Sunday! A fake friend, and I'm so glad I got hip to you."

This music industry thing is changing Bethany and Dreya. Bethany used to be down for me, but now she's so thirsty she can't see straight, and Dreya is taking diva to a whole other level.

Is this going to happen to me, too? Are fame and fortune going to turn me into a monster, too?

26

"Sunday, you've got a letter," my mother says as soon as Dreya and I walk through the door of our Atlanta home from the promo tour.

Her eyes are wide as saucers as she tells me this, like she just walked in on her own surprise birthday party. I just stare at her with a confused frown on my face. I'm completely incoherent from lack of sleep.

The bus ride from New York City to Atlanta took two days total. We stopped overnight in Tennessee, but I still feel like I haven't slept at all. It's a good thing tomorrow is Saturday and I don't have to get up for school, because I would be a total zombie.

But my mother is standing here talking about a piece of mail. I don't know what letter I could be getting that would make her even look all big-eyed like that.

Oh, my God!!!

"Is it my letter from Spelman? Gimme, gimme, gimme, gimme!"

Dreya shakes her head and rolls her eyes. "I'm going to bed. Y'all corny."

" 'Bye, hater."

My mother hands me the letter, which looks frayed and worn but not opened.

"I've been holding on to it for days," my mother says. "But I knew you'd want to be the one to open it."

"Thank you!"

I rip into the paper like it's a Baby Alive on Christmas Day. I inhale deeply with anticipation, but I don't let the air out until I read the first sentence.

" 'Dear Ms. Tolliver, I am very pleased to inform you of your acceptance to Spelman College as a freshman for this fall'!"

"Congratulations, baby!" My mother hugs me and spins me around the room.

"I can't believe I actually got accepted. I didn't think I'd get in this early—I figured I'd have to wait."

"What do we need to do to get your financial aid in order? I want you to go even if I have to take out a loan."

"Mom, I may not need to worry about any of that."

"Oh, really?"

"I wanted to wait until tomorrow to tell you, but I might as well go ahead," I say. "I got offered a record deal."

"You better tell me about this tomorrow. I can't take another announcement tonight," my mother says as she sits down on the couch.

"What's wrong?" I ask.

"Still haven't heard anything from Carlos. I'm starting to think that he might be . . ."

"Don't say it, Mommy. He'll be all right. I know it!"

We sit quietly for a while. I feel sleep descending on me like a heavy, warm blanket.

"Go to bed, Sunday. You look exhausted."

"But I want to tell you about the tour, my record deal, and . . ."

My eyes snap open. "Mommy, did I just fall asleep?"

My mother laughs. "Yes, you did. You should go and lie down. Just leave your bags out here."

I stumble back to my bedroom, with cell phone in hand. I've got to tell Sam about Spelman, and then I'll go to sleep.

I fall into my bed, fully dressed. Dreya is already snoring.

Clumsily, I dial Sam's number in the dark. I'm too lazy to turn the light on and then have to get back up and turn it off again.

"Hello," Sam mumbles.

"Hey, Sam. It's me."

"Me who?"

"Sunday."

"Oh. Hey, Sunday. I'm sleepy. Whazzup?"

"I got into Spelman!"

"Really? I'm so proud of you!"

"Are you really? You don't sound proud. You sound like you're half-asleep."

He chuckles. "I am half-asleep. Can we celebrate over the weekend?"

"Yeah. Call me tomorrow."

"Okay."

I press End on my phone and close my eyes. I want to fall asleep, but my stomach keeps doing flip-flops. I'm in. I'm IN! I'm going to Spelman in the fall. Oh, my goodness.

Too much good stuff happening all at once scares me. I keep waiting for something to go wrong, or to explode in my face.

It's gotta be a dream, right? Well, if it is, please let me sleep for an eternity. I'll be Sleeping Beauty up in this piece!

27

*"Impossible dreams / makin' reality seem / like a
fairy tale / to me. / This ain't make believe /
happenin' to me / like a fairy tale / baby."*
—Sunday Tolliver

My stomach does flip-flops as I sit in the living room
with my mother, Big D, and Sam. I didn't get much
sleep last night, wondering how all this was gonna go
down. I even got up and made my mom orange, mint,
and honey tea, and biscuits out of the can to butter her
up. The record deal needs to happen now, if I want to go
to college and graduate debt free.

My mom reads through the thick stack of papers with
a serious expression on her face. My leg won't stop
bouncing up and down. This whole thing depends on
whether or not she signs the contract.

When I told my mom that Mystique wanted to pay me
and Sam $50,000 for our song, and promised royalties
on the back end, she had to sit down. She didn't believe it
at first. I'm still not sure if she believes it.

Shoot! I don't even know if I believe it.

"Is this what you really want, Sunday?" she finally asks.

I nod. "Mom, you know I love music . . ."

"Yes, I know, but you've been talking about college for so long, and now this?"

"I'm still going to college."

"Ms. Tolliver, if I might explain," Big D says. "Mystique has agreed to Sunday recording her album right here in Atlanta. She can attend class during the week and record on the weekends."

"When will she do her homework, study for exams, go to parties?" my mother asks.

Since when did she care if I went to parties?

"Mom, just look at it like I'm working my way through school. I can do this!"

"And this Mystique is reputable?" she asks Big D.

"She's the real deal, Ms. Tolliver. I wouldn't be so excited about this if she wasn't. She heard Sunday's voice and was completely mesmerized."

"And when will she promote the record? I know that's important, too, right?"

"Ms. Tolliver, you are asking all the right questions! You're a natural stage mom."

My mother laughs out loud. "Well, I just want to make sure no one takes advantage of my daughter, and if she decides to do this, I want her to be successful. She's way too talented to be a one-hit wonder."

"You're right," Big D says. "She'll be much bigger than that. But to answer your question about promotion, she'll be going on tour this summer with Dreya on the Truth and Drama tour. She'll open the show."

"But her album won't be finished by then, will it?"

"Maybe not, but we'll have a few singles ready, and it'll get her name out there."

My mom cocks her head to the side as if she's deep in thought. "So she'll get to promote her records during the summer and go to school during the rest of the year?"

"That's the plan!" Big D says.

Aunt Charlie, who's been sitting on the couch the whole time listening to the conversation, gets a twisted expression on her face.

"I don't hear you sounding this crunk when you talking about Drama's career," she says to Big D.

"Drama is going to be a success, too, Ms. Tolliver."

"Yeah, you better make sure you don't forget it. She's the one who got y'all here. Sunday wouldn't be gettin' any holler if it wasn't for my baby."

"Actually, Ms. Tolliver," Big D says, "we have Sunday to thank for a lot of this. We've worked together as a team, and Sunday doesn't owe Drama anything."

Dreya comes up the hallway looking crustier than a mug, wrapped in a comforter, with her spiky hair mashed on one side. There's a trail of spit going across the side of her face, and her smudged eyeliner is making her look like a raccoon. And . . . she looks like her breath stinks.

"Did I hear you say that Sunday was opening for me and Truth on the summer tour?" Dreya asks in a husky, scratchy-sounding voice.

"Yes, you did."

"How can she do that when she doesn't even have a

record deal? I don't want her on my tour. It's the Truth and Drama tour."

Big D frowns. "You don't get to make that decision, Drama. Epsilon Records along with their sponsors are doing this tour. Mystique wants Sunday on it, and what Mystique wants she gets."

"Mystique?" Dreya asks. "What does she have to do with anything? How does she know Sunday? It sounds like y'all been doing stuff behind my back."

"You're tripping!" I say. "Why do you think I need to tell you about my opportunities? I don't answer to you."

"You're supposed to be my assistant, not my competition," Dreya whines.

Big D says, "Listen. There's room enough for the both of you. Y'all sounds are completely different. Sunday's got that neo-soul vibe, and you're all hip-hop / pop. Actually, y'all complement one another."

"Well, I don't want Epsilon Records to sign her. She needs to get a record deal somewhere else," Dreya growls.

"Sorry, hon. Mystique picked her out personally to be the first artist on her label, Mystical Sounds. You don't have more pull than Mystique," Big D says.

Dreya turns her frown toward me. "You couldn't let me have this one thing, could you? You had to find a way to come up off of my come-up. I hate you!"

She storms out of the room, leaving a trail of hot, stanky breath behind her. It's whatever, though.

"What were we talking about before we were rudely interrupted?" I ask. "I'm ready to finalize this, Mom. What do you think?"

"I think I don't know about you being a celebrity in college. That's gonna make it really hard for you to figure out who wants to be your real friend and who just wants to be with you for the fame."

"I'm not worried about that, Mom. I'm a good judge of character," I reply.

My mother gives me a motherly smile. "You've got it all figured out, don't you?"

"Not everything, but I've thought about it, yeah."

My mother sighs. "Well, I guess since your college fund is gone, and that's my fault, I'm not going to stand in your way on this. But I want them to have a chaperone on tour."

Big D laughs. "A chaperone? They haven't done that since the seventies."

"Those are my rules," my mom says. "If you can't make that happen, I'm not signing this."

"Okay, okay. A chaperone. I'll make it happen. Got anyone in mind?"

"No, but I'd like for it to be an older woman."

I cover my mouth to quiet my laugh at the frustrated look on Big D's face. My mother's making him jump through hoops to get this deal signed. I already know she's gonna sign it, but he's still working hard.

"Okay, Ms. Tolliver. I can do that. Can you please sign the papers before I go into cardiac arrest?"

"Sure, I'll sign it now."

As I watch my mother sign her name in her big, curly handwriting, I feel the butterflies start all over again. It's really going to happen! I'm a recording artist.

The only thing that makes me feel a little bit irritated is Dreya's reaction to this. I can't believe that she wouldn't be happy for me. I was happy for her! I even wrote her some hot songs to make her stuff successful. Why would she be like that toward me?

I guess blood ain't thicker than benjamins.

28

"**O**h, my God! It's Drama!"

The worst thing that has happened since the tour and the appearance on *106 & Park* is the screaming. The constant screaming of girls who used to mean mug in the hallway and now either want my autograph or want to be my friend because I'm Dreya's cousin.

I try to navigate through the majority of the ninth grade (the freshmen are the worst for some reason) to get to my locker. I've got much classwork to make up because of the few days I took off to do the tour.

"Back away from Drama!" Bethany says. "She's got to get to class."

I laugh quietly inside at Bethany's brand-new bodyguard duties. Yeah, I didn't actually laugh out loud. It wasn't amusing enough for all that. All laughter took place on the inside.

What's even funnier is how the kids back up like Bethany

has some pepper spray or a water hose. They don't even fall back like that when the security guards bring the pain.

"Before I go to class, I'll sign two autographs, but you have to show me that you have Truth's single downloaded to your iPod or phone," Dreya says, totally not ready to trade in her adoring fans for class.

Fifty kids start waving cell phones and iPods, trying to get her attention, and she grabs the closest two. Once she's checked their gadgets for the song, she signs a little slip of paper and the back of a notebook. A few flashes come from digital cameras, which aren't even allowed in school. Where is a hall monitor when you need one?

I would feel like a hater on the inside if I didn't know that Dreya doesn't want me to blow up, too. She doesn't want me to have adoring fans, tours, or autograph signings. So it doesn't matter that she's getting on my nerves right now. It is what it is.

Just when I thought I couldn't be any more disgusted by this entire scene, Romell slides up behind Bethany the bouncer and kisses her on the neck. He's still got a bandage on his head from his concussion, but I guess the head injury hasn't bothered his mack game.

"How does it feel to have a celebrity for a cousin?" Katrina, a freshman, asks.

I shrug. "I don't know. My cousin isn't really a celebrity yet."

Katrina frowns. "You should just be happy for her. I saw you on *106 & Park*, too. You wouldn't have been on TV if it wasn't for her."

I want to stand on top of some lockers and scream at the top of my lungs, *The only reason Dreya has a record deal is because of a song I wrote!!!!!!*

Would that be terrible if I did that? Would it make me seem like even more of a hater? I don't know, but her groupies are getting out of control.

Instead of having a hollering tirade I say to Katrina, "You're right. I am happy for Dreya. I think she's really going to go far."

Katrina's frown turns upside down. "That's more like it! I knew you weren't a hater."

I roll my eyes as she prances away over to Dreya's adoring groupie circle. The first bell rings to signal that we have two minutes left to get to class, and the crowd starts to disperse and head in different directions.

I rush into honors English and take a seat next to Margit. She snatches up her high ponytail and straightens it. I smile, because this is Margit's signal that she's about to tell me something.

"You just missed it, Sunday. Mrs. Silo just walked Brandon down to the office. He cursed at her and said he wasn't doing any more essays this semester."

"What? He's crazy. He does know this is honors English, right? Essays are like mandatory."

"I know, right? But he got Ds on his last couple papers. If he gets another bad grade, he's gonna be off the basketball team."

"He's gonna be off if he keeps calling teachers cuss words."

Margit squints and her eyes turn into tiny slits. She flings her long brown hair to one side and leans over to my desk. "I saw you on *106 & Park!* Yay. Is your cousin gonna be a huge star?"

"Not you, too, Margit!"

Can I just have one friend that isn't caught up in this Drama mess?

"You know I really don't listen to rap, but that song is kinda hot! You and Bethany looked good, too, though."

"Thank you."

"Y'all still can't hang with my girl Taylor Swift, though," Margit says with a smile.

"Okay. I'll take that under advisement."

"You're such a nerd, Sunday," Margit says with a giggle.

"So are you! You are sitting next to me in honors English, right?"

"Yeah, I guess. Oh, I got my acceptance letter to Alabama State. My dad is going to be so happy. He played football there."

My eyes light up. "Congratulations! I'm going to Spelman; got my early acceptance letter, too."

"Spelman? I don't know if I could survive no boys on campus."

"There are boys all over the place. The Morehouse men are right across the way."

"I guess. I heard Romell is going to Georgia Tech."

"I don't care about him. I'm going to prom with a guy over at DSA."

"Dish! You haven't told me about any new boyfriend prospects. Is he hot?"

"He's kinda hot, but he's more sweet than anything. And he's talented."

Margit frowns. "So he's not cute, huh?"

"Yes! But he's got that kind of cute that grows on you."

Margit nods. "Gotcha. Starts out kinda ug, but turns on swagger later."

"Yeah," I chuckle. "Something like that."

"Well, that's cool. Am I gonna get to meet him? You haven't been hanging out much lately."

"You'll get to meet him at prom."

"How do you know you'll still be digging him then?"

I shrug. "I hope I am, or then I'll be hunting for a prom date in the tuba section of the marching band."

Margit scrunches her nose. "No, thank you. At least pick a drummer or trumpet player. The tuba boys are always extra large."

"They have to be big to hold up all that metal!"

"No, no, and no. I don't like this mental picture. Hurry and draw me another one."

"Ha, girl. Whatever. Here comes Mrs. Silo."

Wouldn't it be cool if you could just erase situations like you can erase a mental picture? If I could, I'd erase Bethany and Romell flossing in my face. I'd erase Carlos getting shot, and I'd erase Dreya all up out of my come-up.

Yeah, someone needs to invent this mess eraser! Pronto!

29

"Congratulations, Sunday. You stay surprising every-body," Truth says as we chill in the lounge at the studio.

"What you surprised about?" I ask.

"That record deal with Mystique. We on tour and you and Sam having little creep-move meetings with Big D."

"It wasn't a creep move. We wrote a song for her and Big D set up the meeting."

"Well, y'all didn't tell anybody it was going down," Truth says.

I'm trying to figure out what I hear in his tone. Is he mad, jealous, or what? His face is smiling, but his eyes are definitely doing something else.

"The record deal was totally unexpected. Sam and I were just trying to sell her this song we wrote for her."

"It's cool, hustla. You came up."

"Thanks. Your girlfriend isn't happy, though."

"She'll get over it. Shoot, we can all eat."

I give Truth a fist bump. "I'm saying! There's enough room for everybody."

"Y'all don't even do the same kind of music, so I can't believe she hatin' like that."

"She's tripping for real. She tried to tell Big D that she didn't want me on the tour."

"He told me. I got on her about that. You always supposed to have love for your fam when they come up. I don't know what's wrong with her."

Dreya and Big D walk into the room, so Truth and I end our conversation. But not before Dreya caught the tail end.

"You don't know what's wrong with who?" Dreya asks.

Truth laughs. "G'on 'head girl, with all that drama. I ain't in the mood."

Big D holds his hands up. "Time out, y'all. I got some good news about the tour."

Dreya plops down on the couch next to Truth. "The tour that Sunday is crashing?"

"No," Big D says, "the tour that Epsilon Records invited her to join. Stop tripping, girl."

"Whatever." She rolls her eyes at me and flips me the bird. Wow.

"After the crowd went crazy for y'all on *106 & Park*, BET decided to do a reality show on y'all tour. They're sending a camera crew with y'all to every city."

Truth jumps up and hugs Big D. "That's what's up!"

"Wow! That's hot," I say. "We're gonna be hood stars, like *Tiny & Toya* and *The Real Housewives*."

Dreya laughs. "You wish you had it going on like Tiny and Toya."

"I'm good, my family's good, mmm-hmm," I say in my Tiny voice.

Everybody laughs, including Dreya.

"This is hot, especially for you, Sunday, since you'll be in college next fall and can't really do a lot of promo work. They're gonna show reruns of the show all summer, so by the time your album comes out, you'll be a household name."

"We hope," I say.

"Well, it'll happen as long as y'all don't do nothing crazy on tour like get arrested," Big D says.

"So that means I probably shouldn't let my boys roll with us on tour, right?" Truth asks.

"Naw! Your boys have got to roll. Just make sure them cats ain't riding dirty," Big D replies.

Dreya says, "I don't like those reality shows. It's like they try to paint a picture of a person that's not for real. Like I can't believe NeNe on *Real Housewives* is really that full of drama."

"They can only put it on TV if you do it," I say. "So don't act like your usual hating self on the road, and you should be cool."

"Shut up, Sunday."

"Speaking of painting pictures, I think y'all need to capitalize off that love triangle stuff that the blogs started," Big D says.

"What do you mean?" Dreya asks.

"I mean y'all know what's up, so it won't hurt nobody

if y'all play that up a bit. Let them think something is really going on."

Dreya holds up one hand. "I don't even think so. I don't want anybody thinking that my man would want *her*. That's not even believable anyway."

"I think it would be funny," Truth says. "It would definitely have people talking."

"You would want us to do it," Dreya hisses at Truth. "So everybody could think you're some kind of player or something. I don't think so."

"Is anybody gonna ask me what I think?" Sam asks, appearing upstairs from his music lab.

"Why somebody gotta ask you?" Dreya asks. "This doesn't have anything to do with you. You aren't Sunday's boyfriend! As far as I'm concerned, you don't even really have to go on this tour. One less person on the payroll."

"Sunday, you ain't got nothing to say?" Sam asks.

I throw up a hand. "Wait a minute. Y'all don't even need to argue about that, because I'm not doing it. I'm not down with deception. I believe reality should be exactly that—real."

Big D shrugs. "Give it some thought. Y'all got months before it even goes down."

Seriously, Big D? Did you not hear anything we just said?

I don't need to give it any more thought. There is no way anyone would believe I wanted to hook up with Truth. They'd be calling our little show all kinds of fake.

"Oh, I almost forgot," Big D says. "Sunday, tell your

mother that Epsilon Records hired a chaperone. It's Mystique's mother—the fashion designer, Ms. Layla. She does all of Mystique's tour outfits, and this could help her launch her fashion line."

I'm speechless. No, really. I'm utterly speechless.

"I hope she doesn't think I'm wearing any of that tacky stuff," Dreya says. "You'll never catch me in a sequined anything."

"What about you, Sunday?" Big D asks.

"I am not an enemy to sequins, but I would not consider myself their friend."

Truth bursts into laughter. "Don't even look at me."

"Well, *somebody* is going to be wearing Ms. Layla's costumes. We'll figure all that out later."

This tour / reality show sounds like it's going to be a fiasco. Love triangles, sequins, and hateration galore. I'm so excited!

"My girl Bethany's going, right?" Dreya asks.

Her girl? Bethany's moved up in status from her personal slave to her girl? That's too funny.

"I guess she can come," Big D says, "but are you sure she's your girl? I remember not too long ago, y'all was about to bug right here in the studio."

"That makes for good reality TV," Truth replies. "If they start fighting we can just throw some baby oil on them, and they'll look like video vixens in a rap video."

I shake my head, while Sam cracks up laughing. And of course Big D is standing up here pondering the possibilities.

"Bethany and I will not be fighting. I know she's got my back," Dreya says.

Okay, now I'm cracking up, too. I guess they're besties now because they have a common enemy—me.

But it's only a matter of time before Dreya finds out about who's really her enemy, and who's doin' her boyfriend.

30

My mom, Aunt Charlie, Manny, and I are in the living room watching one of Aunt Charlie's favorite movies, *Bad Boys*. Actually, any movie with Will Smith is a favorite of Aunt Charlie's. She calls him her tall, creamy drink of hot cocoa. Yeah, she's corny as what.

"Charlie, next time I'm picking the movie," my mother says. "I think I probably know this movie by heart."

"No, ma'am. You'll have us in here watching *The Sound of Music* or some mess. No, thank you."

"There is nothing wrong with a musical. Julie Andrews gives a wonderful performance."

Aunt Charlie and I look at each other and then both give my mother the hand.

"Forget y'all."

As we watch a car chase with Will Smith and Martin Lawrence, we hear a loud knock on our window. It sounds like someone threw a rock at it or something.

"What the heck was that?" Aunt Charlie asks.

"I don't know!"

Then we hear a loud, ghetto voice screaming from our front porch. "Shawn! Send him out here! Tell Carlos to bring his deadbeat self up outta your house."

Aunt Charlie hollers, "He ain't here, LaKeisha! You betta get up off this property before I put a cap in your behind."

"You don't have a gun," I whisper to Aunt Charlie.

"Shut up! She doesn't know that!" Aunt Charlie hisses.

"Oh, for goodness' sake," my mother says. "I'm going over there."

"Shawn! Last time, they shot Carlos. Don't go over there."

"That girl is not going to shoot me."

My mother goes over to the front window. "LaKeisha, Carlos isn't here. I don't know where he is."

"Don't try to play me, Shawn! I know you riding hard for him. You're the one who gave him that twenty-five thousand dollars, so why wouldn't you help him?"

My mother frowns. "How do you know I gave him money?"

"Shawn, please," LaKeisha says with a cackling laugh. "You know Carlos still deals with me, honey. I don't care how much money you give him or if you let him live with you, he still belongs to me and his daughter."

My mother shakes her head. "Okay, whatever. I'm not about to have a stupid argument with you through my door."

"Why don't you be a woman then and come outside?"

"For what? So we can fight or one of your brothers can

shoot me? I already told you Carlos is not here. If you come back, I'm calling the police on you."

"When you talk to Carlos, tell him that me and my brother are looking for him. They got some unfinished business."

"Whatever."

My mother comes back over to the couch and sits down with a blank expression on her face. "If they find him, I think they're going to try to shoot him again."

"I think you should get a restraining order on LaKeisha," Aunt Charlie says. "She's workin' my nerves."

"Maybe I will."

I rub my mother's back, to try to make that stressed-out expression disappear. "Mom, it's gonna be cool. At least we know that they don't have Carlos. I'm sure he's alive and hiding out somewhere."

"You're right, Sunday. I just have to keep praying for his safety," my mother says.

"When I blow up, I'm gonna move y'all into a gated community so hood trash like LaKeisha can't walk up to our house," I say.

"That sounds good, baby."

"When you *and* Dreya blow up, you mean," Aunt Charlie says. "It ain't all about you, not this time, Sunday."

"What are you even talking about, Aunt Charlie? You and your daughter be on some other stuff."

"I just don't understand why you had to copy Dreya with the record deal. She just couldn't have her own shine, could she?"

"Her own shine? Are you kidding me?" I ask.

"You always get praised for being smart, getting in college, and all that. And as soon as Dreya gets something on her own, here you come trying to steal that, too."

I stand to my feet, totally furious. "I'm sick of y'all trying to act like I stole something from Dreya. I'm the one who wrote the hook that got her the record deal! I wrote all the songs on her record! Why shouldn't I have a shot, too?"

"Listen to you. You're so selfish, Sunday."

"Mom! Are you gonna let her just talk to me like that?"

"Charlie, stop. Let the girls fight it out amongst themselves. We shouldn't even be getting in this. I'm going to bed."

"But the movie isn't even over yet," Aunt Charlie says.

My mother just gets up and walks to her bedroom and closes the door.

Aunt Charlie glares at me. "I'm not gonna let you steal this from Dreya."

"Is that a threat, Aunt Charlie?"

"No, honey. It's a promise."

31

"Can you see me / can you see me? / Tell me what you want me to do / 'cause I wanna see me with you."

I sing the hook to the first song I've written for my album. Big D is bobbing his head and Sam bites the inside of his cheek. This is his thinking pose.

"It's all about a girl who feels invisible to this guy she really likes," I explain.

"I like it," Big D says. "It's so different from what you write for Drama, and it has a different sound from the song you wrote for Mystique. You're a chameleon, girl."

"Each voice is different, I guess. I write for the voices."

"Well, you're doing your thing, girl."

"What will the verses sound like?" Sam asks.

"I've only written the first one. It goes like this: When I first saw you / you were so incredible to me. / All I could do was watch you / a guy like you would never talk to me. / Feels like I'm hiding in plain sight. / Wish you'd just open up your eyes / Can you see me, can you see me? / Tell me what you want me to do / 'cause I wanna see me with you."

Now Sam is rocking back and forth. "That's hot, Sunday!! This has a rock-soul feel and needs some funky drums. Get ready to have a number-one hit."

"You think? I thought it was kind of different. What if people don't get it?"

"People get hot music," Big D says. "It's universal."

"Big D, can I ask you something?" I ask.

"Of course."

"Do you feel like I'm trying to steal Dreya's shine?"

Big D laughs. "You can't steal someone's shine. You either have it or you don't."

"I know! That's what I keep telling myself, but I think my aunt and cousin are getting to me."

"You don't just shine, baby girl, you glow!" Big D says. "And I promise, you're gonna be in this business much longer than your cousin."

I feel myself blushing. "Thanks, Big D."

"When I heard you singing over Drama's vocals and bringing life to those songs, I knew you had something special."

"So why did you present Dreya to Epsilon Records instead of me?" I ask.

"Because it takes someone like Mystique to believe in a talent as unique as yours. They would've never listened to me. Drama, she's typical. She's what they expect from R & B chicks. You are in a class by yourself."

"You deserve this, Sunday," Sam says. "Dreya is just tripping."

"Whew . . . all this praise is making me thirsty!" I say with a chuckle. "I'm going upstairs for water—anybody want something?"

"Nah, I'm good," Sam says.

"I'll take a bottle of water."

I skip up the stairs feeling really good about myself. Big D said that I'm in a class by myself! Sweet!

Truth is standing in the kitchen, making a sandwich, looking pretty darn regular. Not like you would think a rapper on the brink of blowing up would look.

"What are you 'bout to grub on?" I ask.

Truth smiles. "A Dagwood, girl. You don't know nothin' 'bout that."

"It looks like a big ole meat sandwich! You must be hungry."

"I could eat."

"Well, don't let me get in the way. I only need water."

"You know, I was thinking about our reality show," Truth says.

"You got some ideas?"

"Yeah. I think the fans would really like to see us hook up."

I burst into laughter. "Are you for real? What fans? They don't even know who we are yet!"

"But they will. And you're so much sweeter than Drama. I think they'd all be team Sunday."

"Yeah, everybody except Sam."

Here Truth goes again, stepping into my personal space. "You sure you couldn't imagine yourself kissing me?"

"I'm sure."

"Well, I sure could imagine myself kissing you."

I back way up. "Truth, this is not the business."

Truth steps all the way up, cornering me and leaving me no place to escape. He takes my face in both of his hands and gives me a deep, knee-buckling kiss.

"You'll change your mind about wanting to kiss me."

He strokes my face before leaving the kitchen with his sandwich and beverage. I touch my lips that still tingle from Truth's kiss. I can't tell if he's serious or if he's just playing games with me. I know one thing—Dreya wouldn't think any of this is funny.

I look up, and Sam is standing at the top of the steps. How long has he been there? How much did he see?

"Big D wants you," Sam says.

Before I can ask why, Big D yells up the stairs, "Sunday! Come back down here! Mystique is on the phone. She wants to talk to you!"

Mystique calling for me? Get the heck outta here. That's hot!

For the moment, I forget about what Sam did or didn't see and run back down the stairs holding two bottles of water in my hand. I'll do damage control later.

"Here she is," Big D says. "She's on speakerphone, Sunday. Go ahead and say what's up."

I try to catch my breath. "H-hey, Mystique!"

"You sound like you just did a hundred-yard dash," she says in her calm and warm-sounding tone.

"I pretty much did! How are you doing?" I ask.

"I'm great! I just recorded your song, and it sounds wonderful. You are so talented and beautiful, Sunday. You and Sam."

"I don't think I've even been called beautiful before," Sam says. "Thank you, Mystique."

"You are very welcome!"

"I'm glad you like the song!" I say. "I know you're gonna make it a number-one hit."

"This song makes me sound good!" Mystique says. "I appreciate y'all. And good luck on recording your album. I can't wait to hear it."

"Thank you sooo much for this opportunity," I gush. "You can't imagine how much this means."

"Yes, I can! I remember how it felt to get my first record deal."

"I guess you do know. But thank you just the same," I say.

"You're welcome. Okay, I gotta go now, but I'll be calling and checking on you. My mother can't wait to meet you, too!"

"All right, superstar," Big D says. "We'll talk to you later!"

" 'Bye, y'all!"

We all yell good-bye into the speakerphone before Big D disconnects the call.

"That's what's up! Mystique calling you just to say hi!" Big D slaps me a high five. "Get used to it, Sunday."

"How do you get used to somebody like Mystique calling you on the phone?" I ask.

"You will. You'll be getting calls from the entire industry soon," Sam says.

His voice doesn't sound excited at all. He sounds sad.

"Speaking of the industry. Everyone in the A is going

to be at Truth's album-release party next Friday at Club Pyramids. Make sure you're red carpet ready, Sunday."

"Why does it have to be at Club Pyramids?"

Big D replies, "They offered to host the party. Free is always good."

"I guess, but they're a bunch of thugs over there," I fuss.

"That drama is not your drama, Sunday."

"I guess."

Big D puts his arm around me. "Plus, you'll be there with me. I won't let anyone hurt you."

I give Big D a one-armed hug. He's a big guy. But is he big enough to block a bullet?

32

Sam rolls through to pick me up for the release party. We're going to all leave from the studio in a limo, so Sam is gonna take me over there. It feels like we're going to prom!

I went and got my hair done in a tight roller set that's making me look like brown-i-locks or somebody! My dress is banging, too, but it's not something I'd normally wear. I go for comfort, and this skintight silver mini is the opposite of comfortable. But the dress is more comfortable than these stiletto heels.

"Sunday, honey, you look good!" my mother says.

"Thank you."

"Be careful. I don't want you getting hurt by any of Carlos's enemies."

I give my mother a hug. "Mama, you don't have to worry about that! Not tonight. It's gonna be all good."

"Okay. But be safe, anyway. If something pops off, you make sure you're going the opposite direction."

Sam steps through our front door. "You ready?"

"Yes!"

I follow Sam to his SUV and take in his outfit. Jeans, tight shirt, leather jacket, boots. He looks fine as what. I almost wish he was my date for the evening. "You looking hot, Sam," I say before we get into his truck.

Sam spins around and replies, "Like you care."

"What's wrong with you?" I ask. "Why wouldn't I care?"

"I saw you, Sunday. I saw you kiss Truth!"

He *did* see! No wonder he's been tripping.

"You saw Truth kiss *me*. I didn't kiss him."

"I didn't see you pushing him away."

"He caught me off guard. It was over before it started."

"Sunday, I'm not gonna keep diggin' you the way I do if you're feeling Truth. I can't do it."

"I'm not feeling Truth."

"Are you feeling me, though? That's the question."

"Sam . . ."

"You know what, don't even answer. It's cool. Let's do this party, do this red carpet bull, and get this paper."

Sam gets in the SUV and leaves me standing on the sidewalk looking crazy. He doesn't even open the door for me like he always does. I let myself in the SUV.

"Sam, I'm afraid that if we get together during this tour and reality show, we won't last."

Sam rolls his eyes. "Whatever, Sunday."

"No, I'm for real! I don't think it'll work if it gets played out on TV for the world to see."

"Sunday . . . it's cool. I get it, you're on the come-up and you don't want a boyfriend right now."

"Sam—"

"No, let me finish. I haven't been hearing you this whole time, because I keep thinking you're feeling what I'm feeling. But it's obvious that you're not. I'm cool with being friends."

"You're not angry?"

"Naw. Just don't think I'm gonna keep checking for you all like that."

"Okay, but can I ask you a question?"

"What is it?" Sam asks.

"Are you still taking me to prom or do I need to ask one of the tuba players from the marching band?"

Sam sighs. "I want to go to prom with someone who's digging me. So I guess not."

I swallow and look out of the window before he sees the tears in my eyes. I can't believe he's tripping all like this just because he saw Truth kiss me.

"You know I don't want Truth, right?" I ask.

"Sunday, you don't know what you want."

33

Sam stands next to me as we walk down the red carpet at Club Pyramids.

"You're not smiling enough," Sam whispers.

"I am smiling."

"No, you're grimacing."

"That's because my feet hurt."

He laughs. "Why do you have on shoes that hurt your feet?"

"You and Big D made me buy this mess! I knew I shouldn't have listened to y'all."

"You want to go sit down?"

"Yes, please!"

We try to get into the club unnoticed, but Truth sees us. "Y'all come take a picture with me!" Truth shouts over the loud music blaring from the speakers.

Dreya rolls her eyes at me and looks my outfit up and down. She and Bethany look cute, I guess. Bethany has done something to her hair. It's slicked all the way back with a thick, greasy gel that has glitter in it. She's got on a red corset, leather skirt and jacket, and some black fishnet panty hose. Dreya's got leather on, too, but that's her usual. This time it's leather and leopard print put together.

"You look real classy," Truth says as he gives me a hug. "Thanks for coming to my party."

The photographer snaps a few candid photos of me and Truth, and one or two posed photos with the whole group. Sam pulls my arm, I guess signaling to me that he wants to go inside.

"So, Truth," shouts one of the paparazzi, "who is your date for the night? Is it Drama or her cousin?"

Truth laughs out loud. "They both look hot, right? Maybe they're both my dates. Truth can roll like that!"

I shake my head in disgust, and Dreya storms off the red carpet with the cameras flashing the whole way. Truth calls after Dreya, and when she doesn't come back, he yanks my arm and pulls me into a hug. More cameras flash before I snatch away.

"You are tripping!" I say.

"Save me a dance!" Truth says as I walk away.

I ignore him, and follow Sam into the club. Once we're inside, we have to sit in the VIP area because we're underage and can't mingle with the regular club goers.

"Truth is tripping, right?" I ask Sam as we sit down at the table.

"That's what he does. That's his persona."

I lift an eyebrow. "You're cool with what he just did?"

"It's whatever."

A groupie-like chick steps up to the table and smiles at Sam. "You're with Truth's entourage, right?"

"Yeah," Sam replies.

"You want to dance?"

Sam leaps up from the table. "Let's go!"

I can't believe Sam just left me sitting here looking crazy and alone at this table.

"That's what you get for trying to holla at my man," Dreya says as she and Bethany walk up.

"Not in the mood!" I fuss.

They both laugh.

"Come on, Dreya," Bethany says. "You have to get ready for your show."

After a few minutes of me getting pissed watching Sam dance with not one, but two girls, Truth sits down at the table. "You look good tonight, Sunday. You be hiding all that body under them khaki pants and T-shirts. You need to let a brotha see what you workin' with."

"No, I don't!"

"Why you playin' hard to get? You can't be all that into Sam, especially not how he's on the dance floor getting it in."

"I don't care what he does."

"Yeah, you do. It's written all over your face. Why won't you just be his girl? He keeps asking you, and you keep turning him down."

"You don't know anything about that," I reply.

"I think you're waiting on something better," Truth teases. "And I don't blame you."

"Whatever, Truth. Aren't you about to go on stage or something?"

He reaches over the table and grabs both my hands. "I'm for real, Sunday. What I gotta do to get with you? You want me to break up with Dreya?"

Is this dude for real? I feel like everyone in VIP is staring at us as he's holding my hands. The intensity on his face scares me because it makes me think that he really is serious and not just doing this for the publicity.

"You wouldn't break up with Dreya for me."

"Yes, I would. All you gotta do is ask. . . ."

"I don't want you to do anything, Truth."

Truth smiles. "I'ma change your mind about that. That's a promise."

I shake my head and grin. "You don't ever give up, do you?"

"Naw. Come on and dance with me real quick before I have to perform."

He's pulling me up from the table and I almost try to stay in my seat. But then, I see Sam grinding all up on one of those girls like he ain't got good sense. He sure did get over me fast.

I let Truth lead me out to the dance floor, not caring what's gonna jump off. I can't believe Sam is tripping, just because I won't stroke his ego and say I'm his girlfriend. That's really messed up.

Truth puts both his hands on my waist and pulls me close. I close my eyes for a second and enjoy his attention, because he's 100 percent into me.

"You like this, don't you, Sunday?" Truth asks in a gravelly whisper.

I can't answer, because I *do* like dancing with him. He smells good as what and he knows how to move.

Just as I get ready to reply, a commotion breaks out on the dance floor. Wait! I'm right in the middle of it.

Sam has tackled Truth to the floor and lands punch after punch. Truth knocks Sam off of him and jumps up to his feet. He's got a bloody nose, but he's . . . laughing.

"You sure you wanna do this, Sam?" Truth asks. "You gonna give up your career over a girl?"

Sam cracks his knuckles and gets ready to lunge after Truth again, but Big D holds him back.

"Calm down, man. It ain't worth it," Big D shouts. "Truth, go clean yourself up. You've got a show to do."

When Truth is a safe distance away, Big D lets Sam go. Sam storms off the dance floor, but makes sure to give me an angry glare when he walks past.

Big D asks me, "You all right, lil' mama?"

"I don't know. Sam is tripping."

"Yeah, pretty much."

"Do you think Truth will want to have him kicked off the tour?"

"Nah. They're not females, Sunday. They'll get past this and it'll be like nothing changed."

"But I don't get it. Sam just got finished telling me he wasn't checking for me and was dancing up on two girls."

Big D laughs. "And you think he meant it? He just wanted you to say you were his chick. He wasn't trying to give you up."

"And I was supposed to know this how?"

"I keep forgetting how young y'all are. It'll be okay, though."

"How can you say that? With Truth and Sam fighting, the tour is gonna be really twisted. That's not hot."

"Are you kidding me? Did you see all the camera phones catching this fight?"

"I wasn't paying attention."

"At least ten people caught all this action and are probably posting it to YouTube as we speak."

I give Big D a confused stare. "Not seeing how this is helping. If anything, it's making it worse."

"Y'all will get over this by the summer, but check it out. The fight on YouTube is like a commercial for y'all reality show."

"A commercial?"

"Yeah, y'all gonna have every teenager in America tuning in to see how all this drama plays out."

"And that's a good thing?"

"It's a real good thing, lil' mama. I told you before, you've got the golden touch. Or should I say platinum touch?"

I look down at the Claire's bracelet on my wrist and sigh, although I'm sure no one can hear it over the music. How do I fix this mess before the tour?

I've got Sam hating me, Truth sweating me, and as soon as she finds out, Dreya will be on a mission to destroy my life. Big D says I've got the golden touch, but right about now . . . I'm making all the wrong moves.

NOT A GOOD LOOK

Nikki Carter

ABOUT THIS GUIDE

The following questions are intended to
enhance your group's reading of
NOT A GOOD LOOK.

Discussion Questions

1. Sunday has dreams of going to college and becoming an entertainment lawyer. What's your dream career?

2. Who's got more swagger, Truth or Sam? Why or why not?

3. How did you feel when Sunday's mother, Shawn, lost Sunday's entire college fund? If it were you, would you be angry, or would you understand that your mom was just trying to make a come-up?

4. Did Sunday and Dreya play Bethany when they both got record deals and she didn't? Is that just the name of the game?

5. Who deserves the fab life more, Dreya or Sunday?

6. What do you think is next for Sunday and Sam? Are they going to get closer, or will Truth get in the mix?

Don't miss the next book in Nikki Carter's
Fab Life series

All the Wrong Moves

Available in January 2011,
wherever books are sold!

1

—————

"Come on, Sunday. Give it your all. I know you can push this song out."

I take a deep breath and close my eyes. Maybe it's the fact that I'm recording my very first single on my very first album that's got me totally twisted.

Maybe it's the fact that mega-super R & B star Mystique is producing the song and is my mentor! Her words of encouragement are not helping, even though she has a smile on her face.

Mystique continues: "Sunday, I know you've got it in you. I've heard you sing the mess out of this song. Do you need me to leave?"

I shake my head no.

"Do you want me to come in the booth with you?"

I cock my head to one side and shrug. I don't know if that will help, but at this point I'm willing to try anything because I'm tired, hungry, and thirsty.

Sam, the recording engineer and my sort-of crush, says over the microphone, "I'm taking a break. Y'all let me know when you're ready."

I feel the tension leave my body when Sam walks out of the recording room. Oh, no! That's it! Sam is the reason I can't get this song right.

"Talk to me, mama," Mystique says as she steps into the tiny recording booth. "You seem a little stressed today."

I play with my ponytail nervously. "I-I don't know what it is."

Mystique smiles. "I think you know what it is and you don't want to tell me."

"Okay . . . maybe you're right."

"Does it have anything to do with that video on YouTube?"

I sigh at the thought of that video. It was the night of rapper Truth's release party at Club Pyramids, here in Atlanta. It was a hot mess of an evening.

Sam was pissed because I wouldn't be his "official girl," so he was tripping and dancing all crazy on some groupie chicks. Truth, who goes with my cousin Dreya, took that as his opportunity to push up on me yet again, even though I'd told him no a hundred times. But since Sam was acting a fool with the groupies, I acted an even bigger fool and danced with Truth, knowing that Sam would flip the heck out.

And he definitely flipped out.

He bloodied Truth's face up right before his show, and

although the concert went on, the fight was the biggest news of the night. Somebody had used the video camera on their phone to capture the whole thing.

It was on YouTube before we even got home that night.

Ever since then, I've been trying to make it up to Sam. We're supposed to be going to prom together, but it's in three weeks and Sam still isn't speaking to me.

"I guess it has a little bit to do with the video," I admit to Mystique.

"Listen. You guys can't let that stuff get to you. If I got upset about everything that's on the Internet about me and my man, I'd never get any sleep."

"Yeah, but the blogs only have rumors about you! They don't have anything concrete. They've got video of me."

Mystique places a hand on my arm. "It's just your first lesson of being in the limelight. Just remember that someone is always watching."

"That's the problem! I don't know if I want that! I just want to be a normal teenager."

"There are pros and cons to it. But I wouldn't trade it for anything, Sunday! I've traveled the world, met the president, and I have millions of fans that care about me. Do you know I got three hundred thousand birthday cards?"

I laugh out loud. "Wow! Really?"

"Yes. And you'll have the same thing, too. You're so talented, and I know you can do this."

"But this song . . . it's about a girl having a crush on

a guy. It's just hard to do with Sam out there mean mugging me."

"Yeah, guys have pretty fragile egos. He's just hurt right now, I guess."

"But why the double standard? I didn't trip about his groupie chicks."

Mystique chuckles. "From what I heard, you did trip! You danced with Truth? Girl, you know that was messy."

"It was messy, wasn't it?"

"Just talk to Sam. Admit you were wrong, and then maybe y'all can get back to being friends again."

"You think so?"

"Yeah, but I need you to do it quickly, so we can record this single."

Sam walks back into the studio and says over the mic, "You ready, Sunday?"

I glance at Mystique, and she nods. "Sam, I need to make a phone call. Can you hold on a sec?" she asks.

She winks at me on the way out of the booth and mouths, "Talk to him."

I bite my lip as I try to get up the courage to talk to Sam. He seems to be deep in thought as he plays what sounds like random notes on the keyboard. I know him, though, so it's not random. He's got a melody in his head.

I step out of the booth and ask, "Working on something new?"

"What? Oh, naw. Not feeling inspired too much."

"Lost your muse?" I ask.

That was an inside joke, but Sam doesn't laugh. We worked together so well writing the songs on Dreya's album that he'd started calling me his muse. "Yeah, I guess so," he replies.

I clear my throat, trying to think of a way to start this conversation. "Y'all video got twenty thousand hits on YouTube."

Sam gives me a crazy look. Why in the world did I say that? OMG! Open mouth and insert foot.

"Twenty thousand people saw me puttin' work in on Truth. Sweet."

"You're such a guy."

"Yeah. I am."

"You did kinda put a beat down on him, though."

Sam frowns. "Wish I hadn't done it, though. It wasn't worth it."

"I wasn't worth fighting for?" I ask. "Wow."

"Well, why should I be fighting over a girl who doesn't want to be with me? That doesn't make a lot of sense."

"Sam, I never said I didn't want to be your girl."

"You never said you did."

This conversation is going in circles. "So, are we not friends anymore now? 'Cause I still want us to be friends, Sam."

"I guess we can be friends, but you're gonna have to give me a while to get over the whole thing with Truth. When I see him, I just want to punch him again."

"You can't do that! I need . . . I mean, we need you on the tour."

"Y'all don't need me. I'm the studio engineer and producer. I can stay here over the summer."

I touch Sam's shoulder and feel him flinch. "Sam, can you imagine how crazy that's gonna be for me if I have to be on tour with Dreya, Truth, and Bethany without you? As a matter of fact, I'm gonna pull out if you don't go."

"Are you crazy? You can't pull out of the tour. Mystique and Epsilon Records would trip."

"I'm not going unless you go."

"It's not that serious, Sunday."

"Yes, it is."

He sighs. "All right, cool. I'll go."

"Yay!" I kiss Sam on the cheek, and he flinches again. "Don't . . ."

"Friends don't kiss each other on the cheek?"

"I don't want your lips on me."

I give him a smart-aleck smirk. "That's not true. You soooo want my lips on you."

"Sunday, don't play with my emotions."

"Okay, I'll stop. But can I ask you one more thing?"

"What?"

"Are we still going to prom together?"

Sam puffs his cheeks with air and taps a few notes on the keyboard. I can tell he's trying to think of an answer.

"I mean, it's okay if you don't . . . ," I say.

"It's not that I don't want to, but I got so angry with you that I asked another girl at my school to go to my prom."

"Oh."

"You didn't ask someone else?" he asks.

"No. I thought we'd make up by the time prom came."

"Do you still want me to go to your prom with you?"

I shrug. "If you want to, I guess. I don't have a date."

Sam flashes a bright smile. "Okay. We can go as friends."

"Right. As friends."

Mystique comes back into the recording room. "Are we ready to record now?"

"Yes," I reply. "Let's do this."